Summer Reading Grant 2009

Troll's-
Eye View

A Book of Villainous Tales

Other Anthologies by Ellen Datlow and Terri Windling

The Adult Fairy Tale Series

Snow White, Blood Red

Black Thorn, White Rose

Ruby Slippers, Golden Tears

Black Swan, White Raven

Silver Birch, Blood Moon

Black Heart, Ivory Bones

The Green Man: Tales from the Mythic Forest

The Faery Reel: Tales from the Twilight Realm

The Coyote Road: Trickster Tales

A Wolf at the Door

Swan Sister

Salon Fantastique

Sirens

The Year's Best Fantasy and Horror, volumes 1–16

Troll's Eye View

A Book of Villainous Tales

edited by Ellen Datlow
and Terri Windling

VIKING

VIKING   090403

Published by Penguin Group

Penguin Young Readers Group, 345 Hudson Street, New York, New York 10014, U.S.A.

Penguin Group (Canada), 90 Eglinton Avenue East, Suite 700, Toronto, Ontario, Canada M4P 2Y3 (a division of Pearson Penguin Canada Inc.)

Penguin Books Ltd, 80 Strand, London WC2R 0RL, England

Penguin Ireland, 25 St Stephen's Green, Dublin 2, Ireland (a division of Penguin Books Ltd)

Penguin Group (Australia), 250 Camberwell Road, Camberwell, Victoria 3124, Australia
(a division of Pearson Australia Group Pty Ltd)

Penguin Books India Pvt Ltd, 11 Community Centre, Panchsheel Park, New Delhi—
110 017, India

Penguin Group (NZ), 67 Apollo Drive, Rosedale, North Shore 0632, New Zealand
(a division of Pearson New Zealand Ltd)

Penguin Books (South Africa) (Pty) Ltd, 24 Sturdee Avenue, Rosebank, Johannesburg 2196, South Africa

Penguin Books Ltd, Registered Offices: 80 Strand, London WC2R 0RL, England

First published in the United States of America by Viking, a division of Penguin Young
Readers Group, 2009

10   9   8   7   6   5   4   3   2   1

LIBRARY OF CONGRESS CATALOGING-IN-PUBLICATION DATA IS AVALIABLE

ISBN 978-0-670-06141-9

Printed in U.S.A.   Set in Berkeley

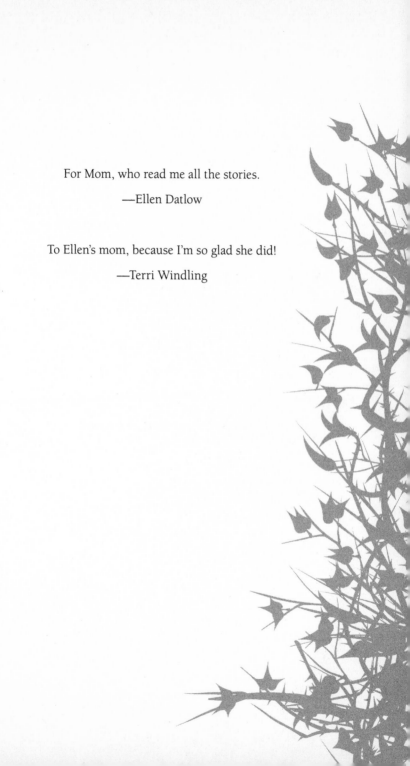

For Mom, who read me all the stories.

—Ellen Datlow

To Ellen's mom, because I'm so glad she did!

—Terri Windling

Contents

Introduction

Ellen Datlow and Terri Windling

We love fairy tales. Not the simple, silly ones found in books for very young children, but the old fairy tales, which were dark, scary, magical, suspenseful, and thrilling, full of cruel stepmothers, malicious fairies, and flesh-eating ogres and giants. In the old fairy tales, no one sat crying in the cinders waiting for a prince to rescue them—they used quick wits and courage to find their own way to a happy ending.

In our two previous books for young readers (*A Wolf at the Door* and *Swan Sister*), we invited writers to go back to the older versions of fairy tales and retell them in fresh, unusual ways. For this book, however, we wanted something new—so we asked our writers to take a long, hard look at fairy-tale *villains*. Witches, wizards, giants, trolls, ogres: what's the truth behind their stories? And are the fairy-tale heroes and heroines pitted against them quite as noble as they first appear? These questions are answered marvelously by the fifteen stories and poems that follow.

Wizard's Apprentice
Delia Sherman

There's an Evil Wizard living in Dahoe, Maine. It says so, on the sign hanging outside his shop:

Evil Wizard Books
Z. Smallbone, Prop.

His shop is also his house, which looks just like an Evil Wizard's house ought to look. It's big and tumble-down, with a porch all around it and fancy carving on the eaves. It even has a tower in which a light glows balefully red at hours when an ordinary bookseller would be asleep. There are shelves and shelves of large, moldy-smelling, dusty leather books. Bats nest in its roof, and ravens and owls nest in the pines that huddle around it.

The cellar is home to a family of foxes.

And then there's the Evil Wizard himself. Zachariah Smallbone. I ask you, is that any kind of name for an ordinary bookseller? He even looks evil. His hair is an explosion of dirty gray; his beard is a yellow-white thicket; his eyes glitter behind little iron-rimmed glasses. He always wears an old-fashioned rusty-black coat and a top hat, furry with age and broken down on one side.

There are rumors about what he can do. He can turn people into animals, they say, and vice versa. He can give you fleas or cramps or make your house burn down. He can hex you into splitting your own foot in two instead of a log into kindling. He can kill with a word or a look, if he has a mind to.

It's no wonder, then, that the good people of Dahoe, Maine, make a practice of leaving Mr. Smallbone pretty much alone. Tourists, who don't know any better, occasionally go into his shop to look for bargains. They generally come out faster than they went in, and they never come back.

Every once in a blue moon, Mr. Smallbone employs an assistant. A scruffy-haired kid will appear one day, sweeping the porch, bringing in wood, feeding the chickens. And then, after a month or a year, he'll disappear again. Some say Smallbone turns them into bats or ravens or owls or foxes, or boils their bones for his evil spells. Nobody knows and nobody asks. It's not like they're local kids, with families people know and care about. They all come from away foreign—Canada or Vermont or Massachusetts—and they probably deserve whatever happens to them. If they were good boys, they wouldn't be working for an Evil Wizard, would they?

Well, it all depends what you call a good boy.

According to his uncle, Nick Chanticleer was anything but. According to his uncle, Nick Chanticleer was a waste of a bed and three meals a day: a sneak, a liar, a lazy good-for-nothing.

To give Nick's uncle his due, this was a fair description of Nick's behavior. But since Nick's uncle waled the tar out of him at least once a day and twice on Sundays no matter what, Nick couldn't see any reason to behave better. He stole hot dogs from the fridge because his uncle didn't feed him enough. He stole naps behind the woodpile because his uncle worked him too hard. He lied like a rug because sometimes he could fool his uncle into hitting someone else instead of him.

Whenever he saw the chance, he ran away.

He never got very far. For someone with such low opinion of Nick's character, his uncle was strangely set on keeping him around. Family should stick together—which meant he needed Nick to do all the cooking. For a kid, Nick was a pretty good cook. Nick's uncle also liked having somebody around to bully. In any case, he always tracked Nick down and brought him back home.

On Nick's eleventh birthday, he ran away again. He made a bologna and Wonder Bread sandwich and wrapped it in a checked handkerchief. When his uncle was asleep, he let himself quietly out the back door and set out walking.

Nick walked all through the night, cutting through the woods and staying away from towns. At dawn, he stopped and ate half the bologna and Wonder Bread. At noon, he ate the rest. That afternoon, it began to snow.

By nightfall, Nick was freezing, soaked, and starving. Even when the moon rose, it was black dark under the trees, and full of strange rustlings and squeakings. Nick was about ready to cry from cold and fear and weariness when he saw a red light, high up and far away through the snow and bare branches.

Nick followed the light to a paved road and a mailbox and a wooden sign, its words half veiled with snow. Beyond the sign was a driveway and a big, shadowy house lurking among the pine trees. Nick stumbled up the porch steps and banged on the heavy front door with hands numb with cold. Nothing happened for what seemed a very long time. Then the door flew open with a shriek of unoiled hinges.

"What do you want?"

It was an old man's voice, crotchety and suspicious. Given a choice, Nick would have turned right around and gone somewhere else. As it was, Nick said, "Something to eat and a place to rest. I'm about frozen solid."

The old man peered at him, dark eyes glittering behind small round glasses. "Can you read, boy?"

"What?"

"Are you deaf, or just stupid? Can you *read*?"

Nick took in the old guy's wild hair and wilder beard, his old-fashioned coat and his ridiculous top hat. None of these things made Nick willing to part with even a little piece of truth about himself. "No. I can't."

"You sure?" The old man handed him a card. "Take a look at this."

Nick took the card, turned it upside down and around, then handed it back to the old man with a shrug, very glad that he'd lied to him.

The card said:

Evil Wizard Books
Zachariah Smallbone, Proprietor
Arcana, Alchemy, Animal Transformation
Speculative Fiction
Monday–Saturday. By Chance and by Appointment

Mr. Smallbone peered at him through his round glasses. "Humph. You're letting the cold in. Close the door behind you. And leave your boots by the door. I can't have you tracking up the floor."

That was how Nick came to be the Evil Wizard's new apprentice.

At first he just thought he was doing some chores in return for food and a night's shelter. But next morning, after a breakfast of oatmeal and maple syrup, Mr. Smallbone handed him a broom and a feather duster.

"Clean the front room," he said. "Floor and books and shelves. Every speck of dirt, mind, and every trace of dust."

Nick gave it his best, but sweep as he might, the front room was no cleaner by the end of the day than it was when he started.

"That won't do at all," said the Wizard. "You'll have to try again tomorrow. You'd best cook supper—there's the makings for scrapple in the icebox."

Since the snow had given way to a breath-freezing cold snap, Nick wasn't too unhappy with this turn of events. Mr. Smallbone might be an Evil Wizard, ugly as homemade sin, and vinegar-tongued with it. But a bed is a bed and food is food. If things got bad, he could always run away.

After days of sweeping, the front room was, if any-thing, dirtier than it had been.

"I've met dogs smarter than you," Smallbone yelled. "I should turn you into one, sell you at the county fair. You must have some kind of brain, or you wouldn't be able to talk. Use it, boy. I'm losing patience."

Figuring it was only a matter of time before Mr. Small-bone started to beat up on him, Nick decided it was time to run away from Evil Wizard Books. He took some brown bread and home-cured ham from the icebox, wrapped it and his flashlight in his checked handkerchief, and crept out the back door. The driveway was shoveled, and Nick tiptoed down it, toward the main road. . . .

And found himself on the porch again, going in the back door.

At dawn, Mr. Smallbone found Nick walking in the back door for the umpteenth time.

"Running away?" Mr. Smallbone smiled unpleasantly, his teeth like hard yellow tiles in his bushy beard.

"Nope," Nick said. "Just wanted some air."

"There's air inside the house," Mr. Smallbone said.

"Too dusty."

"If you don't like the dust," Mr. Smallbone said, "you'd best get rid of it, hadn't you?"

Desperate, Nick used his brain, as instructed. He started to look into the books he was supposed to be cleaning to see if they held any clues to the front room's stubborn dirt. He learned a number of interesting things, including how to cast fortunes by looking at a sheep's liver, but nothing that seemed useful for cleaning dirty rooms. Finally, behind a chair he'd swept under a dozen times before, he found a book called *A Witch's Manual of Practical Housekeeping*.

He stuffed it under his sweater and smuggled it upstairs to read. It told him not only that there was a spell of chaos on the front room but how to break it. Which he did, taking a couple of days over it, and making a lot of noise with brooms and buckets to cover up his spell-casting.

When the front room sparkled, he showed it to Mr. Smallbone. "Humph," said Mr. Smallbone. "You did this all yourself, did you?"

"Yep."

"Without help?"

"Yep. Can I leave now?"

Mr. Smallbone gave Nick the evilest smile in his repertoire. "Nope. The woodbox is empty. Fill it."

Nick wasn't at all surprised when the woodbox proved as impossible to fill as the front room had been to clean. He found the solution to that problem in a volume shoved out of line with the books around it, which also taught him about carrying water in colanders and filling buckets with holes in them.

When the woodbox was full, Mr. Smallbone found other difficult tasks for Nick to do, like sorting a barrel of white and wild rice into separate jars, building a stone wall in a single day, and turning a branch of holly into a rose. By the time Nick had mastered these skills, it was spring, and he didn't want to run away anymore. He wanted to keep learning magic.

It's not that he'd gotten to like Mr. Smallbone any better—Nick still thought he was crazy and mean and ugly. But if Mr. Smallbone yelled and swore, there were always plenty of blankets on Nick's bed and food on his plate. And if he turned Nick into a raven or a fox when the fit took him, he never raised a hand to him.

Over summer and fall, Nick taught himself how to turn into any animal he wanted. November brought the first snows and Nick's twelfth birthday. Nick made his favorite meal of baked beans and franks to celebrate. He was just putting the pot to bake when Mr. Smallbone shuffled into the kitchen.

"I hope you made enough for three," he said. "Your uncle's on his way."

Nick closed the oven door. "I better move on, then," he said.

"Won't help," said Mr. Smallbone. "He'll always find you in the end. Blood kin are hard to hide from."

Round about dusk, Nick's uncle pulled into the driveway of Evil Wizard Books in his battered old pickup. He marched up the front steps and banged on the door fit to knock it down. When Mr. Smallbone answered, he put a beefy hand on the old man's chest and shoved him back into the shop.

"I know Nick's here," he said. "So don't go telling me you ain't seen him."

"Wouldn't think of it," said Mr. Smallbone. "He's in the kitchen."

But all Nick's uncle saw in the warm, bright kitchen was four identical black Labrador puppies tumbling under the wooden table.

"What in tarnation is going on here?" Nick's uncle's face grew red and ugly. "Where's my nephew at?"

"One of these puppies is your nephew," said Mr. Smallbone. "If you choose the wrong puppy, you go away and don't come back. If you choose the right one, you win two more chances to recognize him. Choose the right one three times in a row, and you can have him."

"What's to stop me from taking him right now?"

"Me," said Mr. Smallbone. His round glasses glittered evilly; his bushy beard bristled.

"And who are you?"

"I'm the Evil Wizard." Mr. Smallbone spoke quietly, but his words echoed through the uncle's brain like a thunderclap.

"You're a weird old geezer is what you are," said the uncle. "I oughta turn you in to the county authorities for kidnapping. But I'll be a sport." He squatted down by the puppies and started to roughhouse with them. The puppies nipped at his hands, wagging their tails and barking—all except one, which cringed away from him, whining. Nick's uncle grabbed the puppy by the scruff of the neck, and it turned into a wild-looking boy with black hair and angry black eyes.

"You always was a little coward," his uncle said. But he said it to thin air, because Nick had disappeared.

"Once," Mr. Smallbone said.

Next he took Nick's uncle to a storeroom full of boxes, where four identical fat spiders sat in the centers of four identical fine, large webs.

"One of these spiders is your nephew."

"Yeah, yeah," said Nick's uncle. "Shut up and let me concentrate." He studied each spider and each web carefully, once and then a second time, sticking his nose right up to the webs for a better look and muttering angrily under his breath. Three of the spiders curled their legs into knots. The fourth ignored him.

Nick's uncle laughed nastily. "This one."

Nick appeared, crouched beneath the web, looking grim. His uncle made a grab for him, but he was gone.

"Twice," Mr. Smallbone said.

"What's next?" demanded Nick's uncle. "I ain't got all night."

Mr. Smallbone lit an oil lamp and led him outside. It was cold and dark now, and the wind smelled of snow. In a pine tree near the woodpile was a nest with four fine young ravens, just fledged and ready to fly. The big man looked them over. He tried to bring his face up close, but the young ravens cawed raucously and pecked at him with their strong, yellow beaks. He jerked back, cursing, and pulled his hunting knife out of his pocket.

Three of the ravens kept cawing and pecking; the fourth hopped onto the edge of the nest and spread its wings. Nick's uncle grabbed it before it could take off.

"This one," he said.

Nick struggled to shake off his uncle's embrace. But when Mr. Smallbone gave a tiny sigh and said, "Thrice. He is yours." Nick stopped struggling and stood quietly, his face a mask of fury.

Nick's uncle insisted on leaving right away, refusing to stay for the baked beans. He dragged Nick out to his battered pickup, threw him inside, and drove away.

The first town they came to, there was a red light. They stopped, and Nick made a break for it. His uncle jerked him back inside, slammed the door, whipped out a length of rope, and tied Nick's hands and feet. They drove on. Suddenly it began to snow.

It wasn't an ordinary snowstorm—more like someone had dumped a bucket of snow onto the road in front of them, all at once. The truck swerved, skidded, and stopped with a crunch of metal. Cursing blue murder, Nick's uncle got out of the cab and went around front to see what the damage was.

Quick as thinking, Nick turned himself into a fox. A fox's paws being smaller than a boy's hands and feet, he slipped free of the rope without trouble. He leaned on the door handle with all his weight, but the handle wouldn't budge. Before he could think what to do next, his uncle opened the door. Nick nipped out under his arm and made off into the woods.

When Nick's uncle saw a young fox running away from him into the trees, he didn't waste any time wondering whether that fox was his nephew. He just grabbed his shotgun and took off after him.

It was a hectic chase through the woods in the dark and snow. If Nick had been used to being a fox, he'd have lost his uncle in no time flat. But he wasn't really comfortable running on four legs, and he wasn't woodwise. He was just a twelve-year-old boy in a fox's shape, scared out of his mind and running for his life.

The world looked odd from down so low and his nose told him things he didn't understand. A real fox would have known he was running toward water. A real fox would have known the water was frozen hard enough to take his weight, but not the weight of the tall, heavy man crashing through the undergrowth behind him. A real fox would have led the man onto the pond on purpose.

Nick did it by accident.

He ran across the middle of the pond, where the ice was thin. Hearing the ice break, he skidded to a stop and turned to see his uncle disappear with a splash and a shout of fury. The big man surfaced and scrabbled at the ice, gasping and waving his shotgun. He looked mad enough to chew up steel and spit out nails.

Nick turned tail and ran. He ran until his pads were sore and bruised and he ached all over. When he slowed down, he noticed that another fox was running beside him—an older fox, a fox that smelled oddly familiar.

Nick flopped down on the ground, panting.

"Well, that was exciting," the fox that was Mr. Smallbone said dryly.

"He was going to shoot me," Nick said.

"Probably. That man hasn't got the brain of a minnow, tearing off into the dark like that. Deserves whatever happened to him, if you ask me."

Nick felt a most unfoxlike pinch of horror. "Did I kill him?"

"I doubt it," Mr. Smallbone said. "Duck pond's not more than a few feet deep. He might catch his death of cold, though."

Nick felt relief, then a new terror. "Then he'll come after me again!"

Mr. Smallbone's foxy grin was sharp. "Nope."

After a little pause, Nick decided not to ask Mr. Smallbone if he was sure about that. Mr. Smallbone was an Evil Wizard, after all, and Evil Wizards don't like it if their apprentices ask too many questions.

Mr. Smallbone stood up and shook himself. "If we want to be back by sunrise, we'd best be going. That is, if you want to come back."

Nick gave him a puzzled look.

"You won your freedom," Mr. Smallbone said. "You might want to use it to live with somebody ordinary, learning an ordinary trade."

Nick stood up and stretched his sore legs. "Nope," he said. "Can we have oatmeal and maple syrup for breakfast?"

"If you cook it," said Mr. Smallbone.

✤

There's an Evil Wizard living in Dahoe, Maine. It says so on the sign hanging outside his shop. Sometimes tourists stop by, looking for a book on the occult or a cheap thrill.

In the kitchen, two men bend over a table strewn with books, bunches of twigs, and bowls of powder. The younger one has tangled black hair and bright black eyes. He is tall and very skinny, like he's had a recent growth spurt. The older man is old enough to be his father, but not his grandfather. He is clean-shaven and his head is bald.

The doorbell clangs. The younger man glances at the older.

"Don't look at me," says the older man. "I was the Evil Wizard last time. And my rheumatism is bothering me. You go."

"What you mean," says Nick, "is that you're halfway through a new spell and don't want to be interrupted."

"If you won't respect my authority, apprentice, I'm going to have to turn you into a cockroach."

The bell clangs again. Mr. Smallbone the older bends over his book, his hand already reaching for a pile of black dust. Nick grabs a top hat with a white wig attached to it and crams it over his black curls. He hooks a bushy beard over his ears and perches a pair of steel-rimmed glasses on his nose. Throwing on a rusty black coat, he rushes to the front room, where he hunches his shoulders and begins to shuffle. By the time he reaches the door, he looks about a hundred years old.

The door flies open with the creak of unoiled hinges.

"What do you want?" the Evil Wizard Smallbone snaps.

Delia Sherman has written many short stories and one novel for young readers, *Changeling*. They're all based on fairy tales. She likes doing fairy-tale retellings because she hates making up plots. Even when she's not retelling a specific story, she writes about riddles and animal transformations and the importance of being nice to animals—particularly talking ones.

"Wizard's Apprentice" is a retelling of "The Wizard Outwitted," a Russian fairy tale from *Fairy Tales of Many Lands*, a collection she had when she was growing up. In the original story, everybody knows that the Evil Wizard is evil, but he never really does anything bad—he's mostly just proud and bad-tempered.

This got Delia "wondering about evil and crabby old men and apprentices and transformation." She adds, "I set it in Maine because that's the only place I know where a town like Dahoe might have a chance of existing without anybody noticing."

An Unwelcome Guest

Garth Nix

"There's a girl in the south tower," reported Jaundice, the witch's marmalade cat. "The same one as almost got in last year."

"Well, go and bite her or something," said the Witch. She was busy stirring a huge bronze cauldron. She had twelve coworkers coming for lunch and was mixing up a batch of jelly that had to be poured into an architectural mold and put in the ice cave before eleven.

"Can't," purred Jaundice. "She's in the top chamber."

"What? How did she get up there? I spelled the lower doors shut!"

"She's grown her hair," said Jaundice as if this explained everything, and started licking her paws. The Witch stopped stirring the jelly, ignoring the sudden series of pops as several frogs jumped free.

"How does that relate to her getting into the top chamber of the south tower, pray tell?" asked the Witch sternly.

Jaundice, like all witch's cats, prided herself on her independence and liked to tease her mistress. The Witch didn't usually mind, but she was feeling flustered. The last thing she needed was a girl trespassing on the premises. Particularly a repeat offender.

"She's grown her hair *very long*," said the cat.

She paused to lick her paws some more, till the Witch lifted her ladle and started dripping jelly mixture toward her familiar.

"And braided it into a rope . . . with a grappling hook woven into the end," continued Jaundice, leaping to the Witch's favorite chair, ensuring her safety from dripping jelly.

"She climbed up the south tower using her own hair as a rope?" asked the Witch. "How very enterprising. I suppose I'll have to take care of the matter myself then?"

"It shouldn't be my job, anyway," said Jaundice. "Mice, rats, goblins, and intruders no taller than four feet, that's my province. Not great tall galumphing maidens with ten ells of yellow hair woven into a hawser. She's a sight too handy with that hook, as well. You want to be careful."

"I *am* a witch," said the Witch. She carefully put the ladle aside and began to undo her A COOK'S KITCHEN IS HER CASTLE apron.

Jaundice muttered something inaudible, and her whiskers twitched.

"What was that?" asked the Witch sharply.

"Nothing," said Jaundice. "Just remember I told you about the grappling hook."

The Witch nodded thoughtfully, and instead of taking up the traditional pointy hat she'd got out for the luncheon, she put on her bicycle helmet, and for good measure, added the leather apron she wore when silversmithing. Last but not least, she went to the broom closet and after briefly considering several of her favorites, took out Minalka, a sturdy Eastern European besom with a rough-stained ash handle and a thick sweep of bundled birch sticks.

"You can call up everyone and tell them lunch is off," said the Witch as she greased the broomstick with flying ointment.

"But I want to see what you do to Rapunzel," complained Jaundice.

"Rapunzel," said the Witch. She shook her head, the rat bones woven into her three pigtails clattering on her shoulders. "I knew she had a stupid name. But stupid name or not, you know I can't do anything to her, since she's already inside. Not without upsetting the Accord. I'll just ask her nicely to leave, that's all. You get on with those calls, Jenny."

"Don't call me Jenny!" spat the cat, her back arching in agitation. "My name is Jaundice! I am the evil servant of a wicked witch!"

"You aren't even yellow," pointed out the Witch. "You're orange. And I saw you put that mouseling back in its nest yesterday. Call that evil?"

"I was full," said Jenny, but her heart wasn't in it. She let her back smooth out and jumped over to the telephone, batting off the receiver with a practiced paw.

"And I've never been wicked," said the Witch firmly. "Least, not by my measure. Just independent-minded."

"Wickedness depends on where you're standing, doesn't it?" said Jenny. She thrust out a single claw and started pushing phone buttons. "Want me to call Rapunzel's parents after I've done the coven?"

"Yes!" exclaimed the Witch. Having been born fully adult by a process of magical fission from an older witch, she had no parents and tended to forget such things existed.

"Won't do any good, but I'll call," said Jenny. She winked at the Witch, one emerald eye briefly shuttering, then turned her head to the phone as someone answered. "Hello? Oh, Fangdeath, is that you—"

"Fangdeath?" interrupted the Witch. None of her coworkers was called Fangdeath.

Jenny held a paw over the receiver and quickly whispered, "That's what Bluebell calls himself. You know, Decima's familiar."

The Witch nodded and sighed again, hitching up her

tartan skirt and the leather apron as she straddled her broom. Sometimes she wondered if the familiars regretted entering the Accord, the agreement that had brought peace, order, and security for both ordinary folk and those who either practiced magic, had magic, or were magic in themselves.

Not that the Accord was perfect. There were a few little loopholes, and both sides had been known to exploit them now and again.

This girl Rapunzel had managed to find just such a loophole, and as the Witch flew out her kitchen door and rocketed up toward the south tower, she wondered just what she might be able to do to get rid of her unwelcome guest.

Rapunzel was eating ice cream straight out of the silver cornucopia and watching television when the Witch flew in through the tower window and screeched to a hardbrush landing that scrunched up the carpet and made the coffee table slide into the wall.

The girl put her spoon down and slowly turned her head to look at the Witch. She had to turn her head slowly, because her hair weighed a ton, even with most of it coiled up next to her on the sofa.

"Hello," Rapunzel said brightly. Apart from her ridiculously impossible hair, she looked just like any of the other thirteen-year-old girls that the Witch often saw playing soccer on the oval across the road from her Witchery. She was even wearing her sports uniform, complete with cleated boots. They had probably come in useful for wall-climbing.

"You know you're not supposed to be here," said the Witch. "This is private property and you're trespassing. You have to leave at once."

"Why don't you call the police then?" asked the girl snarkily, her face twisting into a disrespectful moue. "You old bat."

The broom shivered in the witch's hand, Minalka eager to leap forward and smack the insolent brat who had tilted her head on one side and was smirking in a very self-satisfied way.

"You know I can't call your police," hissed the Witch. This was one of the problems of the Accord. If Rapunzel had been detected trying to get into the tower, it would be a matter for the police. But she was already inside, and under the Accord, the ordinary folk's police could not enter the Witchery.

Usually this wouldn't be a problem, as the Witch could deal with intruders any way she liked. But there was another loophole, and Rapunzel knew it and had taken advantage of it. She had not just moved in to any part of the Witchery. She was in the Witch's guest room, and she had eaten her bread and drunk her wine. Or in Rapunzel's case, eaten her ice cream and drunk her lemonade.

From the moment she had done so, she was no longer an intruder but a guest. An unwelcome one, but that made no difference. The Witch could not use magic against her without inviting the retribution of numerous magical entities that defended the guest right with both vigor and cunning.

One of them was watching now, the Witch noticed, from next to the television. A brownie in the shape of a porcelain Labrador. It winked and stuck out its tongue as it saw her looking.

"I think I'll stay for quite a while," announced Rapunzel. She collapsed back into the sofa and picked up the cornucopia and her spoon. "I like it here."

"Why don't you move in permanently?" asked the Witch in her nicest tone.

Rapunzel waggled the spoon at her.

"You think I'm stupid? The second I agree to that, I turn into a housemate, and the second after that probably a toad, right? I'm a guest, right?"

The Witch snarled and looked at the brownie, calculating the odds. It bared its teeth and flicked an ear at the big armchair. The cushion there tilted up to reveal a host of dust-fey, fully caparisoned for battle, many of them mounted on shiny black cockroaches.

The Witch closed her eyes and willed herself to be calm, at the same time tightening her grip on Minalka. The broom had gone beyond wanting to smack Rapunzel. Now it wanted to beat her up.

"Bye-bye, old bat!" mumbled Rapunzel, her mouth full of ice cream. "Don't forget to bring a different cornucopia tomorrow morning, and some clean towels and an extra blanket. Get some more channels for your television, too—this one's pathetic."

The Witch closed her eyes down to narrow slits, to hold back the magical glare that she knew was pent up behind her lids. The brownie and the dust-fey moved and muttered, but the Witch knew they would not attack unless she gave Rapunzel a full Force 10 eyeball assault—which she dearly wanted to do, but knew she could not.

It took some effort to tear Minalka away and aim her at the window, but the Witch managed it. Firmly astride the angry broomstick, she tried to think of some cutting farewell remark, but nothing came, and Rapunzel had changed channels to a music-video station and turned up the volume, a blaring song driven by overcranked bass beginning to shake the room.

The Witch flew out the window and looked at a nearby fluffy white cloud. It immediately became an anvil-shaped thunderhead and began to hail down golfball-sized chunks of ice on the sports field across the road.

Two hours later, the bass from the tower was still pump-ing, and the Witch was still seething. All her nine brooms jiggled and hummed around her as she sat in her favorite chair, and Jenny was curled up on her lap, trying to calm the Witch with a gentle purr.

There had been a brief moment of calm and possibly even hope an hour before, when Rapunzel's parents had shown up, but it hadn't lasted. The girl's father said that he washed his hands of his daughter, that she never listened to him and hadn't for years, and anyway he had to go and milk the sheep or there'd be no speciality cheeses in the shop the next week to keep house and home together. Rapunzel's mother had sobbed and cried and raved about the Witch stealing her little girl away until her husband had shouted at her to face reality and accept that they'd raised a monster, and then both of them had stormed out, leaving the Witch no better off.

"There must be some way of forcing her out without upsetting the guest right," muttered the witch. "A lure of some kind, perhaps."

"Not her," said Jenny. "She knows too much."

"Knows too much," repeated the Witch. "She does,

doesn't she? Far more than any soccer-playing farm girl ought to . . ."

"She reminds me of someone," said Jenny.

"Her hair is too long, too strong," added the Witch. "It's unnatural."

Cat and witch sat thinking, and the nine brooms gently swept around them in a mystic pattern that was possibly conducive to deep thought.

"She's one of the Bad Old Ones come back," said Jenny finally.

The Witch wrinkled her nose. "Possibly. Even if she is, she's still a guest."

"We could ask for help," suggested Jenny tentatively. "I mean, if she is one of the Bad Old Ones reborn . . . we could ask Decima and Nones and perhaps that smith by the crossroad. . . ."

"No," said the Witch. "That would show weakness. I am not weak."

"It would show common sense," said Jenny.

"Shush," said the Witch. "I'm thinking. I can't force a guest to leave, can I? Not unless I want all those under-folk and eaves-dwellers on my back."

"No," said the cat.

"What about if I force a guest to stay?" asked the Witch,

and her lips curled back a fraction, not quite enough to show teeth or be called a smile.

"But we don't want her to stay! How would making her a prisoner . . ." said Jenny, her ears pricking up in sudden attention. Then she did smile, showing her sharp little teeth. "Oh, yes. I see."

Rapunzel was asleep in the Witch's second-best feather bed, when the Brownie licked her face. She sat up at once and tried to slap the porcelain dog, but it ducked under the blow.

"What do you want?" she asked. "Is that old hag up to something?"

"Yes and no," said the Brownie. "I just wanted to tell you that you're not under our protection anymore."

"What?" shrieked Rapunzel. "Why not?"

"The Witch has declared you a prisoner," said the Brownie. "So we're clearing off. Bye!"

The Brownie vanished, and from under the bed there was a sudden flourish of trumpets.

Rapunzel flounced out of bed and ran into the living room, hair uncoiling behind her like an astronaut's tether. Everything was as it had been. She touched the cornucopia and ordered a milk shake and it was there, fresh and cold. The television blared on at the touch of the remote.

"Stupid old fashion disaster," said Rapunzel. "I don't want to leave anyway! There's things I can do here."

She sat on the sofa and wound in her hair, thinking evil thoughts, while animated monsters fought with each other on the television. But after a few minutes, she began to hear something annoying outside. She tried to ignore it, but it just didn't stop, and she thought she could hear her name. Finally she cracked, flicking the television off and flinging open the window.

There was a man at the base of the tower. Or a boy, rather. He was dressed in a red-and-yellow uniform and was carrying a large flat cardboard box.

"Delivery! Rapunzel! Pizza delivery for Rapunzel!"

Rapunzel scowled. The cornucopia didn't do pizza, and she was hungry. She stuck her head out the window.

"Who ordered me a pizza?" she asked. She could smell pepperoni and anchovies, and it was extremely tempting.

The boy looked up. He was slightly odd looking, Rapunzel thought. His ears were a bit long and his hair was white rather than blond.

"We got the prison contract," he said. His voice was high too, and Rapunzel lowered her estimate of his age.

"We do the city jail, the police cells, and now here. How do I get up there?"

"You don't!" snapped Rapunzel. She lugged her hair over to the window and started lowering the braided tresses. She'd taken the grappling hook off before she went to bed. "Just tie this rope around the box and I'll pull it up."

"The pizza'll get mushed up, though."

"Do as you're told!"

"Whatever," said the boy, and shrugged. Even his shrugging looked a bit strange, as if his shoulders were oddly proportioned. "Say, you know, my brothers and I, we do rescues as well as pizza delivery."

"Just tie up the box and clear off," said Rapunzel. Her hair rope was almost at full stretch, dangling just above the boy's head. He reached up and pulled it down. As he grabbed the hair, two other almost identical boys jumped out from where they'd been hiding behind the hedge of thorn bushes and also took hold of the braid.

Rapunzel just had time to brace herself in the window frame before the three boys gave her hair rope a hefty jerk, and she was bent in two, her scalp burning with the sudden strain on her head.

"What are you doing, you idiots!" she shrieked.

"Rescuing you," shouted the three boys, and they hauled on her hair again.

Rapunzel shrieked again, and something inside her, something old and cold and strange that should never have come back to the world, bubbled up from where it was hiding and used her voice to speak a spell. The carefully pruned thorn bushes shivered in answer, and their branches suddenly grew long and the thorns much sharper, and they lashed out at the three boys, scratching horribly, tendrils seeking their pale red eyes.

"Do something!" said Jenny to the Witch. They were both on Ellidra, fastest of the brooms, hovering just behind the corner of the kitchen garden wall.

"I can't," said the Witch. "Not until she's rescued."

"But it's not even her," protested the cat. "It's one—"

"Blind!" screamed one of the boys. He let go the hair and clutched at his face. "I'm blind."

"Pull," whispered the Witch. "Pull! She's almost out!"

The two remaining boys pulled on the hair as hard as they could, even as the thorns scratched at their eyes. Rapunzel clung to the windowsill with one hand and one foot, as whatever was inside her screeched spells and imprecations, most of which were diverted by the charms and defenses of the Witchery gardens.

Then the remaining two boys let go, both with their hands pressed to where their eyes had been. As Rapunzel's hair whipped away from them, one of her stray curses undid the magic that the Witch had used upon them, and instead of three blind pizza delivery boys, three mice scampered in circles, squeaking and crashing into each other.

Rapunzel laughed and began to climb back through the window.

"We'll never get her out," said Jenny despondently.

At that moment, the Brownie appeared and gave Rapunzel a good kick in the back. Completely unprepared, she lost her balance and fell from the window, her nails scoring the bricks as she frantically tried to get a hold.

As she fell, the Witch and Jenny flew over her on Ellidra, faster than any swift or swallow, almost too fast to see. A sparkling powder fell from the Witch's hand, and Rapunzel found herself landing on a great soft coil of hair and she bounced high before landing on her back in the soft earth of a flowerbed.

A second later, the Witch and Jenny landed. The cat leaped from the broom to sink her claws into Rapunzel's chest and the dark shadow there that was trying to sink back below the girl's skin and into her heart. The Witch, brandishing a set of silver scissors she'd made herself long before the Accord had brought peace to the witching world, cut the braid from Rapunzel, very close to the back of her head.

The braid twisted and writhed like a snake and even began to rear up, and the shadow on Rapunzel's chest reached out to it. But Jenny's claws held tight and the Witch's scissors flashed, snipping the braid into shorter and shorter lengths. Finally, the hair moved no longer, and Jenny tore the shadow from the girl and flung it on the ground, where it withered in the sun.

Witch and cat stepped back and both took a breath. Rapunzel sat up and scratched the back of her head.

"Go home," said the Witch.

Rapunzel stood on shaking legs and began to cry. Then she started to run, the thorn bushes arching to make a gate for her exit.

"She'll make the sheep-milking at that speed," said Jenny. "Now where are those mice?"

The Witch held out her cupped hands. Jenny sniffed at them, then retreated back several paces. The Witch breathed upon what she held and whispered a word. Then she bent down and opened her hands, and three fully sighted mice dashed away to a hole in the tower wall, with Jenny not quite close enough behind them.

"Glass of milk?" said a voice near the Witch's foot.

The Witch looked down at the Brownie and nodded.

"I'll pour you one," she said. "Then I think I might go into town."

"Town?" asked Jenny, returning mouseless from the hunt. "What for?"

"I need a haircut," said the Witch, and she shook her head, scowling as her pigtails clashed together.

Garth Nix is the author of two fantasy series for children, The Seventh Tower and The Keys to the Kingdom, as well as books for young adults and adults.

Garth has always had an interest in dark woods, fleeting shadows, and misunderstood eccentrics whom the world has labeled "evil" without attempting to understand their motives. A fan of fairy tales from an early age, he particularly fell in love with a variant of the Rapunzel story called *The Stone Cage* written by Nicholas Stuart Gray. Like all writers, Garth has been deeply influenced by his predecessors, and he describes "An Unwelcome Guest" as "a small but cheerful twig on the great family tree of fantasists, growing somewhere near the towering branches of Nicholas Stuart Gray, Diana Wynne Jones, and Andrew Lang."

Faery Tales

Wendy Froud

When I was young and foolish
and a princess or a milkmaid
or a goosegirl,
I wished for things and got them,
good and bad, gold and toads,
for better or worse,
for happily ever after,
or not.

I slept and woke,
sang among the ashes or was mute,
lived in the tower, the castle,
the cottage,
married my prince, my king
my woodcutter,
lived happily ever after,
my days measured by the

turn of a season, the phase of a moon
and in the end, I died
and in my place, a daughter or a son
or something else entirely
wished, as I had done.

But now, here is the part I like,
where I become the one
to grant those wishes as I please,
and I do.
Snakes and lizards, toads,
diamonds, pearls and gold,
a poison apple, gingerbread,
a pumpkin coach, a gilded dress.
Tools of my trade, my teaching aids.
My gifts, my curses.
Prince to frog, frog to prince,
iron shoes and feet that dance
and dance and dance
and I like it both ways,
like to bless them
and eat them.
Diamonds and blood,
bones and gold.
It's all happily ever after to me.

Wendy Froud is a doll and model maker who has sculpted and fabricated characters for film and television, including *The Muppet Show*, *The Dark Crystal*, *Labyrinth*, and *The Empire Strikes Back*. She has illustrated three books—the Old Oak Wood series—with author Terri Windling, and often works with her artist and illustrator husband, Brian Froud, on book and film projects. Her newest book, which she both illustrated and wrote, is *The Art of Wendy Froud*. Wendy lives in England with her husband, Brian, and son, Toby.

Wendy says, "I wrote this poem because I've often wondered what happened to the young women—the milkmaids, the peasant girls, and the princesses who find their heart's desire at the end of the fairy tale. Who do they become? Perhaps in the end they become those dark characters—the stepmothers, the witches, and the enchantresses—for the next generation of young questing women, choosing in their wisdom to be cruel or kind, benign or malevolent as they see fit. Much more fun."

Rags and Riches

Nina Kiriki Hoffman

Some people live in sunlight, and others of us live in the dark. From the time I was a baby living belowstairs with my scullery-maid mother, I have lived in the shadowed corners of rooms in the castle, though I could see the windows, once I became a housemaid, and the sunlight outside.

The golden-haired princess and her mother, the queen, sat in chairs by the windows, where sunlight fell on their embroidery frames, shone from their silver needles and many colored threads, as they discussed the kingdom's business and added ornament to cloth. I sat with the mending, farther from the light, and listened to everything they said, gleaning bits of gossip to share with my mother when I went downstairs to sleep.

My mother spent her life in the scullery, washing platters and pans, tableware and pottery, but she wanted better for me. "Your father was someone important," my mother said. "A lord he was, though he'd never claim you. You make something of yourself."

She begged sewing lessons from the castle seamstress for me, and that woman worked me hard. I didn't mind, as long as I was learning something new.

My mother asked the other servants to teach me whatever they knew. I was hungry for learning. I was always ready to do jobs others didn't want, as long as I gained new skills. I rose from scullery maid to kitchen maid and then housemaid. I wanted more.

The king had been some years dead. The queen ran the country. In the upstairs sitting room where we all three plied our needles, the queen taught the princess how to run a household and a country, and I listened. If I rose from housemaid to personal servant to the princess, that would be something. The queen treated servants as tools. The princess had a softer side. Sometimes she noticed those who worked around her. Sometimes she gave me a kind word. She was too modest to want her own maid, though the queen had her own attendant and a maid of chambers. I did my best to keep close to the princess, to be the one she asked for help.

When the princess grew old enough to need a husband, rulers in other lands sent proposals to the queen. The queen and the princess studied the proposals.

They settled on one between them, and the next thing I knew, the queen said, "Willa, pack your belongings and the princess's, and prepare to travel to a far country, never to return."

I curtsied and said, "Yes, your highness." Finally I was getting my wish to be the princess's personal servant, though it meant losing everything I had ever known, including my mother.

I folded the princess's many elegant dresses and my three plain ones and put them into the saddlebags, scattering dried lavender among the folds. I wrapped each piece of the princess's jewelry in softened goatskin. I packed the princess's brushes and perfumes and her golden cup, the one she drank from so that no common thing would touch her mouth.

Last, I went down to the kitchen to say farewell to my mother.

"Well," she said, "hear you're leaving us."

"Princess and I leave for a foreign court tomorrow," I told her. "Mam, thanks for everything." I tucked my sewing kit into her apron pocket. It held all but one of the needles and pins I'd filched over the past year, and lengths of thread in different colors, and rolled scraps from the gowns I'd hemmed for the princess and the queen, and just a little piece of gold lace.

She chucked my chin and smiled. "Go find your fortune," she whispered, just like kings instructed their sons in the tales Cook told before we banked the kitchen fires for the night.

Anyone would think a princess deserved a fine carriage to travel in, but not my princess. She had a horse she fancied. Its name was Falada, and it could speak and reason as well as any human.

The queen had assigned us two outriders, young grooms who would lead the pack mules, set up camp for us on our journey, and guard us from bandits. With their help, I loaded all the princess's belongings and food for our journey on the pack mules.

Just before we left, the queen took the princess aside. Queen and princess stood close together, and the queen took a knife to her own fingers and cut the tips until they bled. She let three drops of blood fall onto a white kerchief and whispered to the princess, who took the bloody cloth and slipped it into the neckline of her dress.

It surprised me that the queen would know an old kitchen ritual like that, more that she would practice it.

As we left the castle and the town surrounding it, the princess looked over her shoulder at the world she was leaving behind. I never turned back. Instead I thought of where we were going: into the Forbidden Wood, where anything could happen, or so I had heard from travelers eating their meals in the kitchen.

No one liked to travel through the Forbidden Wood, but the country we were heading for lay just beyond it, and going around would take us three times as long. There was a path through the wood; many people had traveled it safely. All you needed to remember was never to leave the path, not to accept gifts from anyone or anything in the wood, and never to spit into the trees.

The wood wore its spring cloak of new green. The trees grew thick there, with many black boughs against a high blue sky, and the damp, fresh smell of new grass and leaves. Birds called to each other over our heads.

Presently we came to a stream. It ran beside the path in a tangle of stones. A deer lifted its head from drinking and stared at us long enough for the young grooms to pull out their bows. The deer ran then, and the grooms rode off the path after it.

"Wait," I cried, but they ignored me.

"Oh," cried the princess, tugging at Falada's reins, but I caught them before she could follow.

"No, Princess," I said, and the horse said, "No, Princess."

The horse continued, "They forgot the rules of the Forbidden Forest, Princess, but you mustn't."

The forest swallowed the grooms. I knew we would never

see them again. I felt sad, though I had never known them.

We stared after them.

As the last sound of their passage into the forest faded, I turned my horse's head toward the path.

The princess glanced at the stream. "That water looks so cool and fresh. Pray get off your horse, Willa, and take my golden cup and get me some. I'm so thirsty!"

She did look pale and tired, though we had not been more than four hours on the road. I thought about getting her water, and then I thought, *This is the Forbidden Wood, where anything can happen. I want more than I have. I should begin as I mean to go on.*

"If you're thirsty," I said, "climb off your horse and lie by the stream to drink. I'm not going to serve you anymore."

She stared at me, astonished. I, too, felt surprise, not that I had thought the words, but that I had said them aloud.

She glanced around. We were alone, far from anyone who would help her. Finally she slid down and went to the stream. She lay like an animal on the ground and dipped her face to the running water.

After she had drunk her fill, she glanced again at me and murmured, "Heavens, what am I to do?"

The blood drops at her breast spoke. "If your mother only knew, her heart would surely break in two." Their voices were high, and all three spoke in unison.

The queen was a witch! Would the blood drops strike me down for my presumption?

Nothing happened.

The princess led Falada to a rock and mounted her, and we continued through the forest.

The sun dropped from the center of the sky; heat mounted, and shadows lengthened. We came within sight of the stream again, and the princess asked me again for her golden cup. "I'm so thirsty!" she said. "And the stream looks so refreshing!"

"Missy, you don't need my help," I said. "Get your own water. I'm not your servant anymore."

We were neither of us as surprised this time. She slipped off her horse, and said, "Oh, heaven, what am I to do?" Again the three blood drops sang their sad refrain, but they didn't cause me any harm. The princess lay on the ground and drank from the stream, and I saw something white with red on it drop from the neckline of her gown into the water and float away.

The queen's parting gift to her daughter was gone.

Then I knew that I was going to take hold of a new life, for the princess had lost her power. I got down from my horse and walked to Falada. "I will ride you now," I said. The horse stared at me sideways but did not speak.

When the princess finished her drink and rose, brushing dust from her skirt, I brought out the knife I'd slipped into my pocket during my last visit to my mother and said, "I'll take your fine dress now, princess, and you may have mine. Swear on your honor not to tell any living soul what's happened today, or I will kill you."

She was pale and dusty and looked not royal at all, though her hair was still glorious and golden in the late-day sun. I wondered if I could really kill her. Probably not. I wanted a new life better than my old, but I did not think I could buy it with blood. I could spend harsh words, though, and see what they bought. The princess had been careless, but kinder than her mother to me in our old life. I hoped she wouldn't force my hand.

"Very well," she said at last. "I swear on my honor never to tell a living soul what has happened today."

My breath came easier then. A feeling tingled all through me, a strange joy sharpened with worry. I was going to be a princess and find my fortune, just as my mother bade me.

The princess took off her clothes, and I gave her my dress. She even buttoned up her gown on me, and I tied the strings that held my old dress together on her. She got up on my nag without complaint, and I mounted Falada. If the horse bucked me off, all my work would come to nothing, but she didn't. We rode on through the forest. I remembered watching the princess and the queen in all their doings, how they looked when faced with others, what they said with their elevated accents, how their manners made them more elegant. I rehearsed.

Sometimes I spoke to the horse. "I'll treat you just as well as she did," I said. "Promise me you won't tell anyone what I've done."

The horse never answered.

We arrived at the prince's palace on the third day of our journey, and by then I had taught myself to be royal, and the princess acted as though she had spent all her life as a maid. I wore my favorite of the princess's gowns, the deep blue one trimmed with gold lace, the same lace I had given my mother a scrap of. I had tried to make the princess dress my hair, but she was too clumsy, and that was one of my gifts, so I ended up piling my own hair high on my head and fastening it with golden combs. I had attended to the princess's hair as well, braided it tight, coiled it around her head, and placed a cap over it so no one would see its glow.

As we rode into the palace yard, one of the grooms saw us and ran to alert the others. By the time the princess and I stopped, the prince himself had come down to greet me.

"How beautiful you are!" he cried, and reached up to help me from my horse. He had a fair face, fresh, young, unlined by life, and wide, wondering blue eyes. His hair was soft brown, and he was strong, lifting me easily, as though I were a folded sheet or a skein of yarn. He laughed, and I couldn't help but smile at him as he set me on the ground beside him. "My betrothed! Welcome to your new home!"

Strange sweetness ran through me, a taste like honey on my tongue. I had passed for a princess.

"Let me show you to the room we will share when we are married," the prince said. He took my hand and led me into the palace.

The prince had a suite of rooms on the second floor: a bedroom with acres of space in it and large furniture, a water closet, and a sitting room with game boards and tables and books, like the upper room where the princess and the queen had spent time. Two peacock blue upholstered chairs faced each other by the hearth with a table between them. I imagined the prince sitting there with me.

An older man came into the room. He wore a golden circlet on his head. "My love," said the prince to me, "this is my father, the king." I curtsied to the king, but not too low. I was a princess now.

"Well met, daughter," said the king. "Who is that girl you brought with you? You left her standing down below."

"She was a companion on the journey," I said. "I thought I might make a maid of her, but she is not skilled enough.

Is there some job you can give her to keep her busy?"

"I have all the servants I need," said the king.

I thought of the princess turned out into the street, no skills, no calluses. What would become of her? A cold hand touched my heart.

"But I have a boy who watches the geese, and she can help him," said the king.

"Oh, thank you, sir. You are very kind." I dismissed thoughts of the princess.

It was strange being in that great house and never seeing the kitchen or the cellar or the laundry, never taking the narrow back stairs the servants used, never having to carry things for other people.

The prince and I planned for our wedding in two weeks' time. I stayed in a room near the prince's royal suite, and the bed was so soft I had trouble waking. A girl brought me hot chocolate every morning, something I used to do for the princess.

One day the prince suggested we visit a jeweler to look at rings. "Father said I may give Mother's ring to you," he said, "but I thought you might like something new. Should I saddle your horse?"

"My horse?" My horse! I had forgotten Falada! She must be in the stable with the other horses. Had she talked to a groom yet? She had never promised not to speak of what had happened in the forest! "I don't ever want to ride that horse again," I said. "In fact, I want you to have it killed. That horse tried to throw me many times. It's dangerous." I gripped his hands. "Please, my love, have its head cut off."

He drew back from me, staring.

"I beg you," I said.

He kissed my forehead and went away to have it done.

Time carried us all toward the wedding as though we rode a boat on a stream. Every day I felt more solid and comfortable in my new self, and forgot more of who I used to be.

The wedding banquet was to be held the night before the wedding. All the world was invited to celebrate. I dressed carefully with the help of my maid, and did not realize until I was seated at the high table that the prince had not escorted me down to the dining hall.

He sat beside me, but he did not smile. On his other side sat a sun-browned girl in gauzy white, her hair all golden spirals about her shoulders. She seemed shy, half veiled by her hair, her eyes downcast, her face turned toward the lord on her other side, who murmured to her. The side of her face reminded me of someone, but the color of her skin was wrong.

"Who is that?" I asked the prince.

"A friend," he said, but he didn't introduce us.

Tomorrow we will be married, and then I can decide who his friends are. Tonight I will feast.

The old king sat on my other side and watched me eat with a small smile on his face.

After I ate the last bite of my raspberry tart and sat back with a satisfied sigh, the old king said, "I have a puzzle for you, Princess." He spoke loud enough for all the company to hear.

"Yes, Father?"

"What should be done to someone who has deceived everyone? I will tell you the story."

I was tired, dizzy with wine, and too full of food, a little sleepy. I wished there wouldn't be puzzles until after I was married.

"A princess and her maid set out for a distant country," said the king, "and the princess asked the maid to get her water, and the maid said, 'Get it yourself.' The princess asked the maid for water again, and the maid said, 'Get it yourself.' Then the maid said, 'Get off your horse, take off your clothes, and give them to me. I am going to be the princess now. Swear you'll tell no one what I've done or I'll kill you.'"

I had been masquerading so long I had forgotten I wore a mask, but I recognized my own story as the king spoke. I was glad I had had a good meal before they executed me.

"The maid took away the princess's promised husband and made the princess work as a goose girl. A woman of royal blood, tending geese, besmirching herself, restricted to conversing only with servants. That wicked maid, condemning her superior to such a harsh life! What would you do to that worse-than-useless maid if she did such a thing to you?"

I studied the beautiful, sun-touched stranger by my promised husband's side and the princess looked back, directly at me, as she had never done in our former lives. I had always had my head down, saying, "Yes, your highness," when she sent me to fetch something for her or asked me to button up the back of her dress or tend the fire. Now we had both been servants. We had both been princesses. She was the only one who knew both lives the way I did.

"You are foresworn," I murmured.

She shook her head, and candlelight danced over her golden hair. "I did not tell a living soul," she murmured.

"Princess?" said the king to me. "What should be done to such an evil person?" Again he spoke loudly enough that everyone in the hall could hear.

I glanced at the prince, my promised husband, and

saw that he knew, too. He drew away from me, his hand going to clasp the hand of the true princess.

I had lived my dream life as a princess for two weeks only. Now it was over, one way or another. I had traded my whole life for these past two weeks. Still, I didn't regret what I had done. I had slept in a soft bed, eaten fine food, been taken care of as though I were an important person.

The princess touched the golden chain she wore about her throat. She closed her fingers around it and gave me a little nod.

How was I to interpret that? Would she help me or hurt me? Whyever would she help me?

I said, "Such an evil girl should be stripped naked, put in a barrel lined with sharp nails, and dragged through the town by two white horses until she is dead." It was the worst punishment I had ever heard of, one the princess and the queen had puzzled over while they were reading tales of barbaric lands to each other one evening.

"You have pronounced sentence on yourself," said the king.

I looked down at my empty plate. "Yes, I thought you would enjoy it," I whispered to my silverware.

The next day, with great fanfare, all came to see me punished for my presumption. My jailer took me into a tent so I could be stripped and not offend the eyes of the folk who came to watch the punishment, and the executioner brought the barrel in. The nails' wicked points stuck into the barrel.

I had taken off my outer dress and stood in my chemise before the tall, hooded executioner, wondering if I was truly about to die.

The princess slipped under the back edge of the tent. She carried garments in one arm and a bulging burlap sack in the other. The sack's bottom was stained dark, and it made squashy sounds. The princess emptied it into the barrel—slaughterhouse offal, I saw. Then she handed her golden chain to the executioner.

The princess gave her goose-girl clothes to me. With my back to the executioner, I changed into them. We waited together while the executioner nailed the barrel shut with loud blows of his hammer.

While the princess and I peeped past the tent flap, the executioner rolled out the barrel and fastened it with chains to the horses' harnesses. The mob threw filth and rotten vegetables at it as the white horses dragged it through the streets.

We waited until the people had gone, following the barrel's progress, and then we slipped out and headed for a city gate.

"You killed my horse," the princess said as we stood in the shadow of a small, dark gate near the palace.

"Yes," I said. "She would not swear to be silent."

"And in the end, she is the one who betrayed you. I saved her head." The princess nodded, and I looked up, to see the horse's head nailed up inside the gateway. It stared down at me with eyes that looked alive.

"Why would you do such a thing?" I asked.

"I save things," she said. "That's my nature. Falada was my friend, and I couldn't bear to let her go. Every morning, as I passed through the gate, we conversed, and the king, following me one day, heard Falada call me Princess. His suspicions grew from there."

I stared into the horse's liquid eye. If I had granted her a different death . . .

Then again, my own execution had been prevented by the princess.

"Go on, now," she said, and gave me a little push. "You have no place here anymore."

I walked out the gate into the world. I had found my fortune and lost it.

There were other kingdoms, other sunlit skies.

Nina Kiriki Hoffman, over the past twenty-five years, has published many novels and short stories. *Spirits That Walk in Shadow*, a young adult novel, was published in 2006. Nina works at a magazine, teaches short-story writing, and works with teen writers. She lives in Oregon.

About her story, Nina says: "Many things about 'The Goose Girl' fascinate me. How could a horse's head talk after it was cut off? Why would anybody nail it to a gate?

"In the original story, the goose girl princess knew a magic chant that worked: Why didn't she know other magic?

"The maid didn't know any magic, but she knew what she wanted: to be a princess. She made it happen. Unfortunately, she then sentenced herself to a terrible punishment. How could she not recognize her own story when the king repeated it back?

"Maybe she had turned herself completely into a princess in her own mind. Or maybe she had made her dream come true and didn't know what to wish for next."

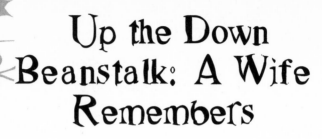

Up the Down Beanstalk: A Wife Remembers

Peter S. Beagle

Special to the Cumulonimbus Weekly Chronicle,
as recounted by Mrs. Eunice Giant,
72 Fairweather Lane, East-of-the-Bean, Sussex Overhead

He seemed like such a nice boy.

And he *was* a nice boy, really, for all the vexation he caused. They always are; I've never eaten a bad one yet. Oh, there's some don't care for the crunchiness, I know that, and there's others who complain about that sort of salty aftertaste. But you clean the palate with a couple of firkins of ale, and where's the harm, that's what I say. No, I like boys just fine. Always have.

The funny thing is that poor old Harvey didn't like them, not really. Oh, he'd eat one now and then, if we were having dinner at someone's house—I mean, you have to be polite, don't you? But for himself, no . . . you could keep that man perfectly happy with a couple of cows, a couple of horses smothered in sheep, the way my mother used to do them—he loved that. Which wasn't exactly what you might call labor-saving, because, after all, cows and horses don't come running to you, do they? I mean, you have to go out and get them, and then you have to carry them all the way home. Not like people—you see what I'm getting at?

It's funny, the way most of them think that boy—Jack, his name was, I keep getting their names mixed up— most of them think that Jack was the first to climb up here. Truth of it is, you can't hardly keep them away. See a beanstalk, they've just got to climb it. It's their nature, I suppose, like kittens with a curtain. Practically all over the place they are, some seasons, what else can you do but eat them? I used to tell Harvey, I don't know how many times I warned him to get that beanstalk trimmed back, so it wouldn't be *quite* so noticeable. But you know how men are, they just put things off and put them off, and then they tell you you're nagging. I think now, if I'd only nagged him a bit more, who knows? Ah, well, mustn't complain.

They tell some story down there, a whole business of magic beans, and trading the family cow to a crafty ped- dler, something like that. Now *there's* nonsense for you. What happened, the cow was wandering loose—whose fault was *that*, I'd like to know?—and Harvey brought her home, so I could have breakfast in bed. Of course that boy naturally followed her tracks right straight to the beanstalk, and maybe he saw her back legs or something vanishing into the sky, that could be. Anyway, he went right up after her and pops into my kitchen, because of the way Harvey trained that beanstalk to grow. I call that clever of him, don't you?

Now, what I always do, I scatter things like rosemary, thyme, salt and pepper, a *bit* of basil, all around that hole in the floor—that way, they're already seasoned, you can just whisk them right onto the grill. But this Jack—my goodness, he was so *quick*! I had to chase him all around the kitchen with a broom, if you'll believe it, before I finally got him backed into a corner. And then—now I *know* you won't believe *this*—the dear boy looks up at me, just as calm as you please, with his little hands on his hips, and he says, "Where's my cow, you thieving giant? I want my cow back!" Cheeky? I ask you!

"I ate your cow on a breakfast tray," I says, "and a tough old thing she was, too. And we'll be having you for lunch, as an appetizer, so behave yourself!" None of that grinding his bones to make my bread, by the by—I mean, who'd ever want to make bread like that, all gritty and nasty?

Anyway. That Jack, he says right back to me, bold as brass, "What about that hen of yours? The one that lays the golden eggs? I'd consider that fair exchange for my cow."

"Golden eggs?" I says. "Golden eggs? Whoever put that in your quaint little head?" The things they believe about us down there! I says, "What would Harvey and I ever want with an egg we couldn't scramble? Now hop up on that grill, and don't be fussing at me so!" Because I was already starting to get one of my heads—you know how I am. It's their voices, I think, that must be it. So *shrill*, they just go right through my temples, but do they care? You've got a hope.

"Well then, what about that harp?" Jack demands—still just as cheeky as he can be. "I know all about that singing harp, and it'll talk to you, too, and tell you the future. Hand it over, and I'll be gone, and we'll say no more about it."

Now you can't help admiring impudence like that, can you? I know I can't.

But. "No harp, no hen," I says, "and if you aggravate me any more than you already have, I'm going to be really vexed with you. I've never known an appetizer to cause so much trouble." I'm sorry, sometimes you just have to be firm with them.

Now all this while, mind you, I'd been moving closer, step by the tiniest step I could manage, me not being exactly built to sneak up on things. But he was too sharp for that;

he zinged and darted around the kitchen like a fly. I hate it when they do that. They never taste nearly as good when they've been overexerting themselves. And if by chance you step on them, or you lose your temper and swat them . . . well, you can just forget it, you know that as well as I do. There is just *no* salvaging a squashed human.

I'd have called for Harvey to help me, but I knew where he was—off with his great boon companion Claude, helping him to fix his septic tank or drain a field, something like that. I have, personally, never been able to stand Claude. He's loud, and he's extremely vulgar, and he's *never* clean, not what you could call clean, and I always thought him a terrible influence on Harvey. But there, try to say *that* to a man, and see what it gets you. The more I expressed my opinion of Claude, the closer friends they became. I should have known better than to say a single word, but honesty's my weakness, always has been. Anyway, I didn't waste any time looking around for Harvey. As much as he and Claude drank when they got together, he'd not have been much use anyway.

But that Jack! I was closing in on him, narrowing down his escape routes—there's a trick to it, I'll show you—but I couldn't ever quite get my hands on him. And *he* couldn't get past me to the hole in the floor, either, so there we were, both just dancing round and round, you might say, and it would have been funny, except that I was starting to get really hungry. It's a blood sugar thing, I think.

"For goodness sake, we can't keep this up forever," I said to him. I was puffing a bit, I don't deny it, but he was losing speed, too, by then. "Why can't we just sit down for a moment and get our breaths and talk like people?"

"Because you're not people, ma'am," says he, not giving an inch. "You're a monster and you'll crunch me up if I take my eyes off you for a solitary minute. Deny it if you can, monster lady."

"I'm not either a monster!" says I, straight back in his face. I mean, that really hurt my feelings, him saying that, as I'm sure you'd have been hurt the same. "I'm big, yes, and I've got dietary needs like you or anyone else. But that certainly does *not* make me any monster."

"Yes, it does, ma'am," Jack says—flat, like that. He still wouldn't let me come any nearer, and he obviously wasn't about to trust me even one pennyworth. So I did the only thing I could do—I just sat down myself, whether he sat or no. Oh, I stayed close enough to that hole so that I could block him with my leg if I missed with a grab. Just in case he really thought we were all as stupid as the stories say.

And by and by . . . well, I won't say he actually *sat*, but he did sort of crouch down on his heels—eigh, dear, what it is to have young legs—and we did chat, in a bit of a way. I asked after his mother, I remember, and about his brothers and sisters—they have them in absolute *litters*, you know—and did he climb lots of things, or was it just beanstalks? Making conversation, that's all.

And he was actually answering my questions, most of them, and even asking one or two of his own, in his cheeky way—would you believe it, he wondered where we ever got underpants in our size—when who should come lumbering in but Harvey! Harvey, with Claude right behind him. Harvey and Claude, laughing and bellowing, with their filthy great boots absolutely thick with mud— if that's what it was—and tracking whole squishy black chunks of *something* all over my nice clean kitchen floor. I could have wept. I just could have wept.

But I didn't. I screamed at them to get out of my kitchen, and of course old Claude was gone the moment I opened my mouth. Harvey was so drunk that he'd never have caught sight of Jack if the boy had only stayed still, but of course he was up on his feet and scurrying along the wall, dodging every which way like a good'un. Harvey let out a yell—"I'll get him! I got him!"—and he made this wild swipe, and Jack actually ran right between his legs, and I couldn't help it, I just wanted to cheer. I'd never tell anybody that but you, but I did! I really, *really* wanted to cheer.

Well, Harvey kept yelling, "I'll get him for you! I'll get him!" but he couldn't have pulled up his own mucky socks, the mess he was, clumping and stamping and scattering more dirt with every step. And that Jack, he could see how distracted I was, and quicker than *scat* he dived for the hole in the floor. Never mind cows, hens, harps, whatever, that boy was on his way home.

And he'd have made it, too, except Harvey somehow lunged and blocked him away, and what happened, Jack lost his balance and sort of skidded on the linoleum. He didn't *quite* fall down, but he was waving his arms, trying to keep his feet under him, and Harvey would have had him in another second. Another second, that's all it would have taken, even for Harvey.

Now I'm not going to swear that I did it out of spite . . . what I did. And I'm not even going to tell you that I did it a-purpose, because I don't know to this day. I *don't*. I'm just going to tell you what happened, which was that Harvey lunged again, and he . . . all *right*, he *somehow* tripped over my foot and went straight down through that hole. Harvey was always tripping over things.

It's a long way down, but we heard the crash. And we stood there, Jack and I—do you know, I never did get his last name?—we stood looking at each other for . . .

minutes? Hours? I've no idea. The boy finally said, "Well. I guess I'll be going."

"And that's it?" says I. "That's it? You break into a lady's house, you call her a thief and a monster, you murder her husband, and now you guess you'll be off somewhere? I thought better of your manners than that, I don't know why. Go on, then, run along with you, by all means. I'm sure *I* don't care."

Jack looked flustered, as he never had when I was chasing him with my broom. "Well, ma'am," he says, "what would you like me to do? I'll surely do what I can to oblige you."

"You could stop for a cup of tea," I answered him straight out. "That's what *civilized* people do when they've killed somebody's husband."

So he stayed on for tea, sitting by the hole with his legs dangling down—a bit rude, I must say, and me too stricken by my loss to have much of an appetite—and we chatted some, and he apologized for saying I was a thief, since it wasn't me stole his cow, and I told him please to give my best regards to his lady mother, and he even helped me clean up a bit, best way he could. He said he'd get the whole village together to bury Harvey, and I asked him to say a few words about Harvey being such a good speller, and a *very* good social dancer, and he said he would. I mean, Harvey had his faults, no denying that, but fair's fair.

No, I haven't remarried, nor likely neither. I'm quite content as I am, thank you, and well enough occupied with my embroidery and my reading. And people *do* keep climbing my old beanstalk, no matter how poor Jack runs all over, warning them not to, so there's any amount of company, and I hardly ever have to eat out. It's princes, mostly—they don't taste any better than anyone else, no matter what you hear—and once there was this whole bunch of dwarves, the dearest little fat fellows. Perfect timing, that was, because my bridge circle was meeting over here that day. So I stay *interested*, that's what's important—being *interested*.

But I do miss Harvey sometimes, I'll admit it. He was always so good at getting the oven going on a cold morning.

Peter S. Beagle has been one of the great names in fantasy for five decades, never quite repeating himself while writing a string of modern classics: *A Fine and Private Place, The Last Unicorn, The Innkeeper's Song, Tamsin,* and the multi award–winning story "Two Hearts."

Peter originally wanted to write about Rumplestiltskin, but that fairy-tale villain was already taken, so he chose his next favorite story instead. "In Western folk literature," says Peter, "guys named Jack tend to be the quick, clever ones—the con artists. Toms tends to be the fools—as in the piper's son who stole a pig and got caught and thrashed for it—the victim, or even the madman, as in *King Lear* and the magnificent 'Tom a'Bedlam's Song.' (Not to mention Tom Tit-Tot, who's a Yorkshire version of Rumplestiltskin.) It's a generalization, of course, but it suited me well enough for my purpose. I wanted to show beanstalk/giant-killer Jack from the point of view of someone who's no fool herself, and who actually gains something from her encounter with a pint-sized cat burglar."

The Shoes That Were Danced to Pieces

Ellen Kushner

I hate being the oldest princess. You always have to be responsible and watch the younger ones, and make sure they have their shoes on before we leave, and that Serena doesn't forget her scarf so she doesn't catch a chill, and Imelda takes her asthma medicine so she doesn't wheeze, and Larissa has eaten properly so she doesn't faint, and keep the twins from fighting.

And that's just at night. We still come home in the morning with our shoes all danced to pieces, so tired we can hardly hold our heads up at breakfast. So then Father wants to know why Juliana is so pale, and why can't Georgina stop yawning like that? And he turns on me with, *Cara, you're the eldest, you're responsible, why don't you look after your sisters properly?*

Well, I tried, didn't I?

They are the worst sisters in the world. They all get to do whatever they want, all eleven of them. When I was little, I had to be in bed with lights out by sunset. But now even little Netta gets to stay up almost as late as the rest of us. That night I'd just gotten her tucked in when all my other sisters started throwing pillows around and dancing like idiots, making fun of each other and fighting over whose turn it was to sleep in the bed with the carved gryphons, and Chandra and Serena started jumping on the bed, and of course Chandra fell right over and hit her head against the biggest gryphon's beak. There was a horrible crack, but it wasn't her head, it was the sound of the floor sliding open underneath. We all rushed to see—and there were stairs, going down, down, down, leading who knows where.

"Me first!" cried Juliana. She's always climbing apple trees, and it's a wonder she hasn't broken her neck. Whenever I tell her to come down, she sticks out her tongue at me. When I said no one was going down those stairs, she did it again.

Georgina always copies her. "Try and stop us."

"I'll tell Father!" I said, but they all started in with, *Father's not here. Don't be a scaredy-cat, Cara. You're no fun. You're just like a wicked stepmother, you're not our sister at all, Cara. Come with us or we'll have all this fun without you and you'll just get in trouble anyway, so there!*

I followed them down the stairs, trying to make sure

no one slipped and hurt herself. Netta, the youngest, whimpered softly because she's afraid of the dark but she doesn't dare admit it. I took her hand, and she snatched it away.

"I'm not a baby!"

But as we went down the next step, she grabbed me and wouldn't let go until we got to the bottom. And there was a magical kingdom with twelve princes waiting, one for each of us. They invited us to a banquet up at their castle lit with torches over the lake. I didn't think we should go, but the others were already scrambling into the boats, so I had to follow to make sure nothing happened. I am responsible, after all.

The food was good, I must admit, and the music was wonderful. We danced and danced, until our shoes were worn out, and so were we. Then we got back in the boats and went up the stairs and into bed, and about ten minutes later it was time for breakfast, with everyone yawning.

The next night, they went down the stairs again, so I had to go with them. And the next, and the next. Dancing and parties are fun once in a while, but I knew this wasn't good for any of us. Besides, who were these princes? I wasn't even allowed to *meet* any princes when I was little Netta's age, and here she was dancing with one, night after night. Where did they come from? If we asked, they just laughed, and twirled us around. I begged my sisters to stop. Once I even planted my feet on the top step and said I wouldn't go.

"But it won't be any fun without you!" my sisters whined.

I knew they didn't really want me to go with them. They don't think I'm fun at all. They never ask me to play or tell me secrets or anything, because I'm the oldest. They were just afraid I'd tell on them. But if they went, I had to go, too.

Getting them all into bed used to be a nightmare. But now, my sisters could hardly wait for the maids to blow the candles out, because the minute they did, they were pulling their dresses out from their closets, and doing their hair in new and interesting ways, and binding their shoes and sleeves with fresh ribbons. And we'd go dance until the soles of our shoes wore right through, and the ribbons holding them on were all gnarled and tangled. It wasn't fair. I didn't even have my first pair of real dancing slippers till I was fourteen, and then I had to beg for them! My sisters all got theirs right away for their first dance lessons.

"See?" they said. "It's fun, Cara!"

They may have had fun at night, but during the day

they were a nightmare, cranky and mean, even to each other. Imelda stole Larissa's drawing pencils and said Honora had done it. Rosa actually cut the hair off of Netta's favorite doll, and Netta cut a big chunk of hers off in revenge.

I thought they'd realize then, but it only made them worse.

"Don't tell," they'd whisper over breakfast, pretending to pass me the salt. *Don't tell* when they combed my hair. *Don't tell.* . . . And to make sure I heeded the warning, one day there was sand in my bed, the next a hole in my cloak, then my favorite embroidery gone missing, even the book my godmother gave me left out in the rain.

Of course, Father didn't notice any of it.

He did notice, finally, that each of us had ordered a dozen pairs of new shoes for dancing, because the maids were complaining that our old ones were all worn to pieces every morning.

So at night he started locking the door to the big room we all slept in. But it didn't make a bit of difference, and he realized that, too.

And so he brought in the princes.

Regular princes, the sons of regular kings who just wanted to make a name for themselves by solving the mystery and winning a bride (plus half the kingdom). Every night, for three nights each, a different prince camped out beside our door so he could follow us when we escaped, learn where we went, and stop us.

But the poor things didn't stand a chance; they were sound asleep, thanks to a potion Chandra always mixed up and put in their wine.

After a month of ten princes at three nights each (each of whom had to be welcomed and feasted before he failed and left), Father announced that the next man who tried and failed would be put to death.

When they heard that, my sisters just laughed.

Things had gone too far. I couldn't be responsible for all those men, as well as my horrible sisters.

That morning I took out the cloak my godmother had given me, an old woman's cloak that smelled like lavender, with a deep, deep hood. I took out her other gifts, too, and snuck out of the palace, and made my way to a crossroads, and sat and waited for the right one to come along. I sat for a long time before someone stopped: a man with brown hair, and ragged clothes, and those little lines you get around your eyes if you stay in the sun too long, or laugh too much, or both.

"Good morning, old grandmother," he said. "You look weary. Is there anything I can do to help you?"

"Good morning, my lad," I replied in a creaky old lady

voice, keeping my face hidden. "It's kind of you to ask. You look like you could use some help yourself. See that castle over there . . . ?"

I gave him good advice and a few other things, and just hoped he wasn't too proud to use them.

Then I went home and took a nap.

That night, who should Father bring to our room but a common, ragged-looking fellow?

"What's this?" said Honora. "Run out of princes to spy for you, Papa?"

"Not at all," our father huffed and puffed. "Plenty more where they came from. But what use are they? Just fall asleep, and then they'll have to be killed in the morning. Bad for foreign relations. No, princes were a bad idea. This is your new guard, my dears. A real soldier. Been in the wars and everything. Trained in combat and the martial arts. Right, Bob?"

"It's Cobb," the soldier said softly. "Yes, your majesty."

"Nobody gets past Rob, here." Our father clapped him on the shoulder. "He'll protect you. I want to make sure nothing happens to my twelve precious darlings," Father said. "Not to mention the price of all those shoes! Right, Nob?" The soldier just nodded.

"Now you just make yourself comfy in this chair, here

by the door—but not too comfy; don't want you falling asleep!" Our father held up his huge key. "I'll lock you all in for the night. Sleep tight, girls, and don't get up to anything!"

The soldier sat down in the chair, and there he stayed, staring at the door.

The twins couldn't keep away from him. They are such flirts. "What are you doing?" Mara asked.

"Thinking," the soldier said.

"What about?" Tara asked.

"None of your business," he said, nicely but firmly. It was a little rude, but they deserved it.

"Now girls," I told them sweetly, "bedtime!"

"Cara," said Honora sharply, "aren't you going to offer our distinguished guest some wine?"

"Yes," mocked Rosa, "you are the *eldest*, after all. It's your *responsibility* to be polite."

I poured wine from our special bottle and offered it to the soldier.

"Oh no, my lady. I never drink on the job."

"Don't be a bore," I said in my best grown-up princess voice. "A little wine never hurt anyone. Here, I'll have some with you."

Well, of course I faked it as usual; I just pretended to drink mine, but he knocked back the full goblet. And sure enough, pretty soon he was snoring fit to beat the band.

As soon as they heard the snores, my sisters were all out of bed like a shot, poking and falling all over each other in their haste to get out their best and prettiest dresses and help each other put them on. When everyone was dressed, Chandra tapped the bedpost, right on the Gryphon's beak.

The Gryphon opened his eyes. "Yes?"

"The usual," she said smartly, and the Gryphon stretched his wings and nodded. The bed began sinking into the earth. There below it was a long narrow set of stairs. The girls all rushed toward it. "One at a time!" I reminded them. "Don't slip!"

We held on to the wall in the dark. Netta was last in line. I heard her cry out, "Quit it, Larissa!"

"What?"

"Quit stepping on my dress."

"I did not!"

"You did so!"

I looked back. "Netta, don't be an idiot. How could Larissa have stepped on your dress? She's in front of you, not behind you."

"Well, *somebody* did," Netta sulked.

"It wasn't me."

"Will you girls shut up?" Honora snapped. "You probably just stepped on it yourself."

I could have sworn I heard laughter then. But it wasn't any of us.

Finally we got to the trees. I just love the silver trees. They stretch out alongside the alley, giving a quiet, shining light as you walk between them.

It was so beautiful and peaceful—until we heard the bang: a loud cracking noise, right over our heads. Rosa screamed, "A gun! Someone's shooting at us!" And half my sisters were clutching at each other and screaming, and the other half were breaking off silver branches and flourishing them like swords, shouting, "Villain! Show yourself!" which was not very helpful.

"Quiet!" I yelled. "Quiet, you fools! It's just the guns up at the castle, firing off a salute to welcome us."

"Or to make sure you don't get lost," muttered Honora.

But we came to the golden wood next, right on the path. We walked on, unusually silent, under the golden branches with their golden leaves. And there it was again: one sharp cracking noise. Everyone jumped, even me. And then I remembered. "That's your stupid prince, Rosa. He's always going on about what a sharpshooter he is. He's probably doing target practice to impress us."

"Shut up," Rosa said. "He's a lot smarter than your prince. Cuter, too."

"You should be glad you're here, Cara," Imelda chimed in. "You're so old and ugly, no normal prince would ever want to marry you."

I didn't answer them.

"Ouch!" Imelda cried. "Who pulled my hair?"

But nobody had. "You must have caught it on a branch, Imelda."

The leaves above us turned to diamonds. They clustered like acorns on the trees.

Crack!

"It's ghosts!" squealed Netta.

"I'm scared," Mara whimpered.

"Me, too," Tara sniveled.

Sometimes I could just knock all their little heads together till their brains (what they have of them) run out their little noses.

I was never so glad to see the lake in all my life.

It glowed with the light of two dozen torches, two in each of the boats of our dozen princes. And the lights of the castle on the other side were reflected in the water, too.

Prince Galahad helped me into our boat. He has a fine profile, which he always turns to me as he rows us across the lake. He never speaks; he is lofty and silent. Not like that little snot of Netta's, the curly-haired prince who throws spitballs at the others, and one time we caught him trying to braid Mara and Tara's hair together behind their chairs at the banquet. Him. Over the splash of oars I heard him say in his loud, obnoxious voice, "My sweetest Princess Netta, I swear on my honor you are getting as fat as a whale!"

"I am not!"

"Then why does this boat weigh so much? I can barely move us in the water."

"So what?" Netta sulked. "I am not fat."

Beautiful and aloof, Galahad took my hand, and led me up the torchlit path to the castle, to the dance.

The music was loud, trumpets and drums, loud and hard and demanding. The princes all twirled us and spun us, and we jumped and leapt in their arms from one to another. We danced hard, and we danced long, longer than we ever had before. Each time I held out my hand, there was someone waiting to grab it and to partner me. I felt a rough hand, once, calloused like a workman's. But all I saw was the same twelve princes, dancing with my sisters and me, on and on throughout the night, high and low, slow and fast, while the drums pounded our beat and the trumpets dared us to stop. We danced the slippers right off our feet, till there was nothing left of the soles but shreds, and the ribbons to tie them on.

That was when we had to stop. Without a word,

everyone knew it. Each prince took one of my sisters' hands and led us down to the boats. The rowing was slow, oh so slow. This time my own boat sat low in the water, and Galahad strained at the oars (though of course he said nothing). I sighed—and again I heard it, that little, low chuckle of laughter, as if someone agreed with me that it had been a very tiring night, but still, it was too bad it had to end.

On the shore I let Galahad take my hand. "Good-bye," I said. My heart was pounding. "Until we meet again." I heard my sisters hissing behind me their warning: *Don't tell.* "Don't worry," I said. "All will be well."

We all dragged our tired feet back through the forests of diamond and of silver and of gold and climbed the stairs back to our room. The soldier was slumped by the door, snoring peacefully. I patted the Gryphon's carved golden feathers. "Good night," I said, and the floor slid noiselessly back into place. We helped each other out of our dresses and dropped our shoes on the floor by our beds and got under the covers and slept.

But it would never be the same again.

Our father summoned the soldier to report the next day. Imelda heard about it when she went back to our room to get her embroidery scissors, and she told Rosa, who told all the rest of us, "Come on! Let's see the soldier get his pay!"

We hid behind a door and heard our father say, "Well, Robbie. The princes got three chances, but you're just a common soldier. You can't expect to get the same kind of treatment as a prince, now can you?"

"No, your majesty," Cobb replied in his soft voice.

"Now, Hob, then, here's the question. Ahem!" Our father cleared his throat. "Where do my twelve daughters go at night, and how do they dance their shoes to pieces?"

"I can't tell you that, your majesty."

"Too bad, my boy, too bad."

At my side, Larissa whispered, "Too bad he's going to be dead."

"But I can show your majesty."

"Can you, now?"

It was agony. We could hear, but we couldn't see through the door what Cobb was showing him. We knew it was bad when our father roared, "Send for my daughters! At once!"

We tumbled through into the study, all twelve of us. We stood in order of height, and curtseyed to our angry father as perfectly as we knew how, but it didn't help. Our father the king was furious.

"Girls," he shouted, "is this true? Do you go out dancing every night in an underground kingdom with strange men?"

All my sisters looked at me.

"No, Father," I said. It wasn't really exactly a lie. They weren't strange; we knew our princes very well by now.

"Well, then, how do you account for this?" He held up a branch of silver leaves. "And this?" A gold one. "And *this*?" The diamonds. "And *this*?" It was a cup from the banquet.

There was only one explanation. The soldier must have followed us. He hadn't really drunk the wine at all. He'd been right behind us the whole time, invisible, treading on Netta's dress and weighing down her boat, breaking off leaves in the woods with a sharp *crack*, even dancing with us at the ball. But how? Someone had warned him and given him the magic to make it work. Someone had given him good advice, and he had not been too proud to take it.

"Bob here saw it all," the king said. "And you can't deny it. Your dancing nights are over. Not to mention all those shoes."

Serena screamed. Imelda started wheezing. Larissa fainted. Rosa burst into tears. Netta threw herself on the floor and kicked her heels and howled.

Father glared at me. "How could you let this happen?" he raged. "You're supposed to know better! You're the eldest. You're responsible! Can't you keep them in line?"

"No, I can't!" I shouted back at our father, the king. "Nobody can! You can kill every prince in the world, but they'll still be spoiled, evil little brats. . . ."

To my horror, I found my nose and eyes starting to prick with tears. I couldn't let those tears out. I mustn't cry, not in front of them.

The soldier said, "Now, let's all calm down. It was like this, see: I was walking, tired and hungry, and I met an old woman by the side of the road. It was she who told me to come here and try my luck, and how I might succeed. My mother always taught me to respect old ladies, and now I guess I know why. She told me how to stay awake, and gave me her Cloak of Invisibility so I could follow them."

My father brushed his hands together. "All right, my boy. I hadn't quite planned it this way, but I gave my word, and a king's word is law. You're now entitled to half my kingdom and one of my daughters' hands in marriage. Claim your bride."

My sisters crowded together, whimpering and clutching at each other. They wanted princes, not some common man with calloused hands.

"Which one?"

Father sighed, with a glance at little Netta. "I suppose you'll want the youngest and prettiest. Princes always do."

"I'm not a prince," said Cobb.

"Doesn't matter," Father said. "Just take your pick."

We all looked at him, holding our breath.

"I'll take the eldest, then. She's got sense."

I squared my shoulders and stepped forward and took his hand.

"Oh, no!" my sisters wailed. "No, no! You mustn't!"

"Yes, I must," I said calmly. "He might need help running the kingdom."

The soldier smiled at me. I saw that the lines around his eyes were laugh lines.

"And besides," I added, smiling back, "I *am* responsible."

Ellen Kushner grew up in Cleveland, Ohio, and loved fairy tales and pretending to be other people. She wanted to be an actress, but someone told her actresses needed to dance, and she was convinced she was a terrible dancer, which turned out not to be true, but by the time she found that out, she was already a writer and a radio host. (Her program is called *Sound & Spirit*.) She has written fantasy novels for adults and one book for young readers, *The Golden Dreydl*. She lives in New York City.

"I have two younger brothers. But even though I'm the eldest, I had to sit in the middle seat in the car—right on the hump!—every time my family took a trip, to keep my little brothers from killing each other. We finally discovered that if I told them a story it would quiet them down. I don't think this is what turned me into a writer, but it did give me lots of practice in making up interesting things on the spot. This story is based on 'The Twelve Dancing Princesses,' which was always one of my favorites. It is dedicated to all oldest children everywhere, who are responsible whether they want to be or not."

Puss in Boots, the Sequel

Joseph Stanton

In the aftermath, the cat's out of the bag.
No longer content to be a clever slave

to a clueless master, Puss lands on his feet—
his hostile takeover so smoothly engineered

that his former master barely discerns
his own dismal, sudden passage back to rags

and the cat's ascension to the dream
his cruel intelligence has earned—

the vast estates, the naïve kingdom's crown,
the gorgeous, cat-adoring queen.

Joseph Stanton writes poems about things he loves. *A Field Guide to the Wildlife of Suburban O'ahu* comments on the plants, animals, and people he enjoys observing on the Hawaiian island where he lives. *Cardinal Points: Poems on St. Louis Cardinals Baseball* celebrates his favorite baseball team. *Imaginary Museum: Poems on Art* describes the paintings he likes best.

He is now writing poems about fairy tales. Joseph wrote about "Puss in Boots" for this book because he thinks that the smart cat in that story would outsmart even his master. He thinks this because he has a cat at home named Kenny who always outsmarts everybody in his family. He had to get the cat's permission to publish this poem.

The Boy Who Cried Wolf

Holly Black

There's a certain kind of boy that likes to read only about things that have really happened. Like Alex. He read about the *Titanic* and memorized how many people died (1,500 to 1,523) and the name of the boat that picked up the survivors (RMS *Carpathia*). He read about ghosts and werewolves too, sometimes, but only when he was certain he was being presented with facts. (The vulnerability to silver bullets, for example, was made up by modern fiction writers—probably any bullet would do.)

In one of the books Alex took out of the library, there was a story about a white flower, the scent of which turned people into wolves. He worried about the flower. It seemed to have no proper name for him to memorize.

In the summers, Alex's parents took him and his younger sister, Anna, sailing. For two weeks, they slept on scratchy cushions in a tiny room in the prow of the boat. Alex mostly sat on deck, his skin tightening with sunburn even though it was slathered with coconut-smelling lotion, and his hair stiffening with salt as he read. Sometimes the glow of the sun on the paper was almost blinding.

Anna swung around one of the stays. She'd been running around the deck all day in a red bathing suit and a floppy hat, dancing up to him and trying to get him to play games with her. Meanwhile, Dad fished off the back and Mom steered lazily. There was barely any wind, and the swells were small. Alex was bored but comfortable.

"Want a plum?" Mom called, reaching into a cooler.

"Nah," Dad said. "Alex just wants to sit there with his nose in a book. All this beautiful nature around, and he doesn't want to experience any of it."

Alex ducked under the mast and took the fruit, frowning at his dad. He bit into it as he resettled into the cockpit. The plum was mealy and less sweet than he thought it would be. The juice ran over his hand.

The book on Alex's lap was about sharks. He imagined them darting beneath the boat, sleek and hungry. Mako sharks were the fastest—but pelagic, meaning they liked open water. They seldom surfaced. According to what he had read, the great white shark could swim anywhere. In any kind of water. He kept his eyes on the waves, looking for thin, angular fins.

Sharks would eat anything. He considered dropping his plum over the side. He bet that so long as it was moving, a shark would eat it. It was the movement that enticed them.

If one did come, then Alex would tell his family what to do. Alex would be a hero. Even his dad would think so.

"Mom," Anna said. "When can we swim?"

"When we anchor," Mom said.

"When will we anchor?" Anna asked, the whine in her voice more pronounced.

"Depends on the wind," Dad said. "But it won't be more than a hour."

"You said that an hour ago," said Alex, but he didn't mind. He liked reading about sharks with all that deep water underneath him.

In a little over two hours, they anchored off a lagoon in Jamaica. They'd flown into Montego Bay a week ago and had been working their way down the coast. Most nights they inflated the dinghy and rowed in for ginger beer and dinner at one of the little fish places along the shore. To-night, though, there was no town, just a lagoon and Mom, boiling potatoes in the galley.

The beach was nice. No coral to cut up their feet. Anna paddled near some rocks, picking up snails and trying to catch the little lizards that seemed to be everywhere. She chased one into the water and then scooped it up, triumphant.

Alex walked on the beach, looking for shells. Dad scooped sand out of a hole, ready to start a fire and grill the grouper he'd bought the day before. Mom's potatoes finished boiling, and she brought them over, wrapped in tinfoil, to stick in the fire.

That was when Alex spotted them. The white flowers.

They grew among the scrub, near a banana tree crawling with ants. Tiny buds of white on long stalks. Like the pen-and-ink illustration in the compendium about werewolves. He wasn't sure, but what if they were the *same kind*?

In the story, two children had been out picking flowers when they stumbled on the white ones. After gathering a few stems, they turned into wolves and raced home to eat their parents.

What if Anna picked one? Alex imagined her sprouting fur and how upset his parents would be, how convinced that she would never hurt them. When she went for Dad's neck, Mom would still be sure that Anna was only attacking because she was scared.

But what if Mom or Dad were the ones that picked a flower?

He'd have to run for the flowers, smell them fast, and hope that he turned into a wolf, too. But it was too easy to imagine if fast wasn't fast enough. He thought of sharks.

"Hungry?" Dad called to him.

His stomach rumbled in answer, and he felt sick.

What if the scent could blow to them? What if they didn't even need to get close to the flowers?

He wanted to tell his parents about werewolves and have them row back out to the boat, but that plan would never work. Dad didn't believe the facts that Alex read if they contradicted his ideas about things. *Just because it's in a book*, he was fond of saying, *that doesn't make it true.*

Alex could just imagine his father sniffing the flower to prove his point.

Anna ran up to where Dad was cooking the grouper. Her legs were covered in sand and she had a hooded cover-up on over her bathing suit. "Is it almost done?" she asked.

The fire lit her eyes. As he looked at his father and mother, he saw the flames reflect in their eyes, too. He shuddered.

What if he went and sniffed the flower first? Then *he* would be the wolf. Then he would have no reason to be afraid. And if he started turning, he could tell them to run and get off the beaches before he finished transforming. He would know what was happening. He would be *experiencing* nature.

And if the flowers weren't the flowers from the book, no one would know he'd made a mistake or that he'd been so worried about his own family eating him up.

He took a step toward the flowers. Then another. He imagined the scent of them drifting to him, a combination of his mother's perfume and sweat. That couldn't be the real smell.

"Alex," Mom called. "The food's done. What are you looking for?"

"Is there a lizard?" Anna asked. She was heading toward him.

"No," he said. "I just have to pee." That stopped Anna.

The white flowers blew in the breeze. His heart was beating so hard that he felt like he couldn't catch his breath, like each beat was a punch in the chest. He reached for a bud, pulling it free. The plant sprang back, petals scattering. He brought the single flower to his nose, crushing it, inhaling sharply.

He was hungry, hungrier than he could remember being in a long while. He thought of the plum and tried to remember why he hadn't finished it.

"Wash your hands in the ocean when you're done," his mother said. Alex was so surprised by her voice that he dropped the blossom. She didn't know what he was doing, he reminded himself.

Ripping the plant out of the ground, he shredded it. Just to be safe. Just to be sure.

He walked back to the fire, waiting for his skin to start itching. It didn't.

Alex ate two potatoes, three ears of corn, and most of the tail of the fish. He felt good, so full of relief that when Anna bounced up to him in the light of the setting sun and wanted to play tic-tac-toe in the wet sand, he agreed.

She drew the board in the sand and made a big X in the middle. "Okay," she said. "Your turn."

He drew an O in the upper left-hand corner. Their mother was gathering up the plates to take back to the boat. He wondered if she was going to make dessert. He was still kind of hungry.

Anna drew an X in the bottom right corner. He hated going second. One of the facts of tic-tac-toe is that the person who goes first is twice as likely to win as the person that goes second.

Looking at Anna's red bathing suit through the hooded cover-up made it seem like he could see past her skin to the raw meat underneath. His stomach growled, and Anna laughed. She found every gross body sound to be hysterical.

"Come on, kids," their mother called. "It's too dark to play."

He looked up. There was only a sliver of a moon. The sun had slid all the way under the water.

Alex's stomach cramped, and he winced. He thought about the fish, sitting in the ice chest all day. Maybe it had gone bad.

Anna laughed. "You should see your face. Your eyes got really big. Big enough to—"

His hands cramped too, curling up into claws. Anna stopped laughing.

"Mom!" he yelled, panicked. His vision shifted, went blurry. "Mom!"

Anna shrieked.

"What's the matter?" His mother's voice sounded close, and he remembered that he was supposed to warn them.

"Get away!" His voice broke on the last word as another wave of pain hit him. "Stay away from the flowers!" That made no sense. How was she supposed to understand that?

He opened his mouth to explain when his bones wrenched themselves sideways. He could hear them pop out of sockets. His scream became a howl. Fur split his skin.

New smells washed over him. Fear. Food. Fire.

Anna came into focus, racing across the beach toward their father. He could feel his ears lift, his mouth water. He leapt up onto all fours.

Sharks were right. It was the movement that was enticing.

"*Alex,*" his mother said, bending down, reaching toward him. As if he would never hurt her. His gaze went to her throat.

"Laura!" his father shouted. "Get away from that animal! Where's Alex?"

Alex opened his mouth to answer, but the words came out a growl, low and terrible. The quick flash of terror in his father's face made him salivate. He had to run. Before. Before. Before something happened. Banana leaves brushed his back and he nearly tripped over long banyan roots. He kept moving, his nose full of rich scents. Lizards. Beetles. Soil. Salt. He was so very hungry.

Just keep running, he told himself. Like a shark through deep water.

Alex tried to think of all the things he knew about wolves. They could travel long distances. They hunted in packs and howled to demonstrate territory but barked when nervous.

His red tongue lolled as he panted.

None of those facts meant anything anymore.

He came to a house in the woods with a roof of corrugated metal. An old woman with salt-and-pepper hair hung brightly colored sheets on a line. She sang as she worked. A basket sat beside her, full of laundry. She looked so kind, like someone's mother, someone's grandmother. His mouth watered and he crept closer.

She might be someone's grandmother, but at least she wasn't his.

Holly Black is the author of several contemporary fantasy novels for children, teenagers, and whosoever else might like them. The books include the best-selling series The Spiderwick Chronicles, as well as *Tithe, Valiant,* and *Ironside.*

When she was a child, Holly's parents forced her into long vacations on their sailboat, where she dreamed of turning into a wolf and devouring them. Fortunately for them, she never did turn into a wolf, and even if she had, seasickness probably would have rendered her too queasy to eat anyone.

Troll

Jane Yolen

Troll peeked out from under Bridge just as the sun was setting. It was raining.

"O, I like rain," Troll said. Of course he said the same about fog and wind and sleet. "O, I like fog." And "O, I like wind." And "O, I like sleet." He was that kind of troll.

His name was simply Troll and he had no other. His Mother had little imagination when it came to names, or anything else. Lack of imagination is why you so seldom see Trolls today. Except on the Internet.

Troll was like his name: heavy on top and bottom with a kind of round O philosophy of life. Meant he was hard to tip over and hard to surprise.

Troll's Mother had said to him one bright summer day, "Troll, dear, I am going above (meaning on top of Bridge) and get us Goat for supper." She had said this before, of course. Often. And every time it was the same. She'd be gone for a bit and then return, with Goat for supper.

But this time it was different. This time she never re-turned. There was a splash. And a crash. But Troll, having no imagination, could not fathom what that splash and crash meant. So he waited and waited, but his Mother never returned.

Troll was simple and had no imagination, but he was not stupid. He knew that his Mother's disappear-ance had something to do with Goat, since that was the last thing she had mentioned, and he was determined to have nothing more to do with that horrid creature—for supper or otherwise.

So he took to eating Grass and Reeds and the occa-sional Fish. The Very occasional Fish. It was not a big River.

"O, I like fish," he would say often, though not—I am afraid—often enough. He grew up pretty stunted for a Troll, which means he was only about twice the size of a grown Man instead of quadruple in all directions.

Now it was the first spring without his Mother, and there was plenty of green Grass on either side of Bridge. Under Bridge was becoming noisy, what with the spring spate and Water tumbling over Rocks and the increase of trit-trot-traffic over Bridge. Troll could scarcely sleep in the daytime for the noise, and it made him grumpy. Even a small Troll grumpy is not a pleasant thing.

Troll growled and muttered, he fidgeted and fussed,

he whinged and whined and wrangled his considerable hands. Even his O became misshapen and ugly.

"Ooooow, I do not like noise," Troll complained. "I do not like it at all." He made a swipe at a small speckled Trout that laughed at him, escaping on a trail of bubbles far downstream. To make matters worse, when Trout was far enough downstream to feel totally safe, she flipped up into the air and zinged a frothy raspberry in Troll's direction before heading toward the sea.

"Ooooow, I hates Fish," Troll said and, for that moment, it was true.

So for the next few days, Troll ate no Fish, but subsisted on Reeds and Weeds. He got light-headed from the lack of protein and his stomach growled all the time. In fact it growled so much, no one in the neighborhood was aware of the oncoming Storm. Goats still gamboled over Bridge, and everyone laughed at Troll and his growly tummy.

Goats sang a song as they went over Bridge that went something like this:

> Troll's tummy
> Is rumbly-rummy.
> Isn't that funny.

which is why Goats are not recording artists or poets or

even considered particularly literate. And Bridge hummed along. But then it was a Bridge after all.

And then Storm actually rumbled into the neighborhood, shouting and shaking and sending down Lightning in great zigzag strikes that hurt Ground wherever it landed. You would have thought the neighborhood wits would have been wary. But they were still convinced the noise was just Troll being cranky. And a little Troll at that.

So Storm blustered in, making loud comments no one listened to and shaking his fist at the surroundings, with no one the wiser. One particularly large Goat, with horns as big and sharp as gaffing hooks, was at that very moment trit-trotting over Bridge. He'd added a verse all his own to the song about Troll, which only went to prove how silly Goats are:

> *Troll's belly*
> *Is really, really smelly.*
> *It smells like h—*

He was about to say a swear, of course, which his sainted Mother—if she'd still been around—would have washed his mouth and beard out with good carbolic soap for uttering.

But Goat never got a chance to say that final word

because his huge horns stuck out and attracted the attention of Lightning, the way a rod on a house does.

Before anyone—Goats, Bridge, or Troll for that matter—could warn him, the big Goat was fricasseed, roasted, toasted, and fried. Pick your favorite Goat dish. I know which one I prefer.

The smell was delicious.

Troll sniffed that smell and his rumbly tummy flipped right over with delight. So he followed the smell to the top of Bridge and found a meal waiting for him, crisp on the outside and juicy beneath.

"O, I like This," Troll said, though he had no idea what "This" was, because he had no imagination. But he *could* tell it was food. So he ate and ate, the grease running down his chin, until he was absolutely and embarrassingly full, his tummy stretched as tight as a drum. A big bass drum, not a little bongo. And then his tummy stopped rumbling.

Storm moved away over Mountain at the same time, so nobody knew the difference between Troll's rumbling tummy and the grumbling Storm. But from then on, everyone in the neighborhood thought that a thunderstorm meant Troll was on the hunt.

And maybe he was.

After all, Troll spent the rest of his life grabbing up any

Goat who trit-trotted over Bridge to get to the good green Grass on the other side. Goats always live with the idea of hope triumphing over knowledge.

And Troll lived that way, too, always hoping to find a repeat of that wonderful taste, with the crispy, crunchy crackling and the drippings that ran down his chin. He never did, of course, since Trolls had not yet discovered Fire.

But it was not for lack of trying.

Moral: *If at first you don't succeed, invent fire. Or hire a chef. Preferably one with imagination.*

Jane Yolen, who has more than two hundred eighty books to her credit—including the Caldecott-winning *Owl Moon*, illustrated by John Schoenherr—has always loved fairy tales. In fact, growing up, she read all of Andrew Lang's Color Fairy Books, which included folktales from around the world.

"Then," Jane says, "I loved the princes and princesses. Nowadays, I find the villains more interesting. Trolls, poor things, always get kicked around. So for this book I chose to write about one of the most famous trolls in history. Note that the word *story* is the back end of the word *history*. There's a reason for that!"

Castle Othello

Nancy Farmer

"You'll never guess what's happened," said Lady Trephine at dinner. The table had been placed on the balcony, for it was a breathless summer night. Only two torches illuminated the balcony, and they were placed as far away as possible.

"We already know. The news was all over the market-place," her older daughter informed her.

"You shouldn't be gadding about the marketplace," said Lady Trephine, annoyed at having her surprise spoiled. But she was too excited to stay angry. Someone had bought the entire hill on the other side of the valley! The new owner had already brought in a hundred men to clear trees and build a palace.

Lady Trephine narrowed her eyes at her two daughters. Anne, the older, was sharp-tongued and intelligent. Felicia, on the other hand, was as sweetly dull as a ripe fig. Their mother smiled inwardly. Since when had *dull* mattered in the marriage market?

"Is he noble?" said Felicia, gazing across the dark valley. The Trephines were so blue-blooded, not a single man
in the neighborhood had been good enough for them.

"Someone that rich must surely be noble," Lady Trephine said. "He has imported the finest stonemasons and
gardeners."

On the whole, Lady Trephine liked living alone with
her daughters. Ever since Lord Trephine had died, her
days had been peaceful, with no nasty-tempered husband
dragging in slaughtered deer and wild boar. Her sons
Arturo, Rodrigo, Fidelio, and Giovanni also loved hunting, but they had their own houses. Lady Trephine sighed.
She must not be selfish. There were few enough marriage
possibilities for Anne and Felicia.

"I shall send the gentleman a dinner invitation as soon
as he moves in," Lady Trephine said.

The new palace was surrounded by a high wall. The
workmen said it contained many rooms built around a
courtyard, a most delightful place filled with orange and
almond trees. A procession of carts brought finely made
furniture, tapestries, thick carpets, and every other luxury.

But as yet no one had seen the owner of the palace.
There was only his deputy, a near-giant of terrifying ap-
pearance who gave orders. When the rear of the building
was finished, it was sealed off. This excited great interest.

All believed these rooms were filled with treasure, for in the darkness of night, carriages arrived and their contents were never seen.

"They say he's a Venetian prince," said Lady Trephine. "He won a sea battle and captured plunder so rich it took a hundred men a hundred days to remove it."

"I heard in the marketplace that he murdered his wife," remarked Anne.

"Don't repeat such lying gossip," cried her mother, "especially where Felicia can hear it." But Felicia wasn't listening. She was dreaming about the hundred men carrying sacks of gold for a hundred days.

Eventually the workmen finished their tasks and were sent away. Anne watched from a high window for the approach of their new neighbor. With monotonous regularity, Felicia would call up the stairs, "Anne, sister Anne! Do you see anyone coming?"

And Anne would reply, "You asked that question five minutes ago. Stop bothering me."

But one day she saw a cloud of dust in the distance. It resolved into a troop of soldiers, carrying banners and followed by a long line of carts, carriages, and slaves. The girls raced down into the village. Cages of brightly colored birds were carried past. Musicians blew trumpets. Jugglers tossed balls into the air. Acrobats performed cartwheels. It was the most exciting display the villagers had ever seen, and they all cheered wildly.

Until the lord of the castle arrived. The villagers fell silent. He was as tall as a doorway on his great black stallion. His chest was as wide as a kettledrum, and his beard was so black it glinted blue where the light caught it. His skin—

"He's a *Moor*!" wailed Felicia, falling into her mother's arms when she got home.

"He rides well," observed Anne.

"Yes, but he's a *Moor*! Of all the rotten luck!"

"It's worse than you think," said Lady Trephine. "I had already sent an invitation to his palace before I heard the news. He has answered most graciously—for a Moor— and will be here tonight."

Felicia took to her bed, but Anne gallantly helped her mother plan the meal. The evening went well in spite of the younger daughter's refusal to speak or even look at their guest. Lord Othello was well educated. He had been a prince in Morocco, before being enslaved by Christian corsairs. His captors did not send him to be worked to death in the galleys, as most Muslim slaves were. They presented him as a gift to Pope Leo.

The Pope had been delighted, and freed Othello at once. Leo had found a soul mate in the Moorish prince.

Both men enjoyed luxury and lavish parties, and there was no question Othello was a charmer. He was endlessly inventive, planning festivals, setting up a zoo, importing fireworks from China. He introduced the pontiff to amusements that had never been seen in Rome. Or at least not in public.

Unfortunately, Leo had died, and his successor favored the Inquisition. Pope Adrian turned Leo's pleasure palace into a leper colony, and painted over the delightful murals Othello had commissioned in the bedroom.

The Moorish prince had departed and made his way through several small Italian kingdoms, staying a year or so in each, until he arrived in Venice. There he became commander-in-chief of the army.

"Why, with such success, have you traveled to our little backwater?" Lady Trephine inquired.

"One tires of fawning adulation." The Moor smiled broadly, his white teeth gleaming in his dark face. "I crave a quiet existence, where one may enjoy the pleasures of marriage."

"Oh! Have you brought your wife?" Anne said brightly.

The Moor smiled again. "I had hoped to supply myself with such a treasure here. I find city women too bold. Give me a simple village lass to lavish jewels upon."

Felicia glanced up and quickly down again.

"You would do me great honor to visit my palace, noble ladies," Othello continued. "Please bring as many companions as you please."

Lady Trephine's worries were laid to rest by the mention of companions. No mischief could occur in a crowd and besides, she was consumed with curiosity about what lay behind the palace wall. "I would be delighted," she replied.

That night, after Othello went home, Anne said, "I have heard in the marketplace that he had to flee Rome. Furthermore, he also fled Genoa, Milan, Pisa, Naples, and Venice. Do you suppose he murdered a wife in each of those cities?"

"Rich men always attract gossip from the jealous," said Lady Trephine irritably. "It ill suits you to repeat it."

The palace was more exquisite than anyone could have imagined. Everything was decorated with gold or crusted with jewels. Felicia admired herself in a tall mirror—the first ever seen in the village—and Lord Othello amused himself by fastening pearls around her chubby neck. "You have made the mirror happy by bestowing your beauty upon it," he murmured. Felicia giggled.

Hunts were arranged in the forests nearby for Lady Trephine's sons, as they were bored with such things as culture. But for the ladies it was one long week of pleasure.

Actors performed plays in the garden, while silent-footed slaves carried around trays of sweetmeats and sherbet. Minstrels sang. Acrobats teetered in pyramids that almost—but not quite—reached the top of the high walls. A monkey wrestled a bear cub. Oh, there was nothing like the entertainments of Lord Othello! Felicia and Lady Trephine were enchanted.

"Perhaps his beard is not quite so blue," Felicia whispered to Anne.

"I wonder what he's hiding back there," Anne said, looking at a door that had not been opened. "Perhaps the bodies of his murdered wives."

"Anne!" cried both Felicia and Lady Trephine.

Felicia and Othello's marriage was celebrated with a week-long party and all of the villagers were invited. Everyone agreed that Felicia's husband was a splendid fellow—for a Moor—and that she had been extremely fortunate.

But when all had departed, the new bride found herself often lonely. There were the slaves (who never spoke) and the tame deer, kittens, performing monkeys, and so forth, but Othello himself disappeared for three weeks out of every month. Where did he go? She didn't know. She would merely wake up and find him missing.

Felicia had never been good at entertaining herself.

She had depended on Anne, and now she found the days unbearably empty. Furthermore, Othello never allowed her to leave the castle. She was used to running to the marketplace for this and that. She enjoyed the admiration of the young men lounging by the village fountain. Of course she never encouraged them—well, not beyond raising a skirt to show an ankle, but what was the harm in that?

Once, out of boredom, she dropped a handkerchief to see a handsome slave pick it up. Othello flew into a rage. He tore the handkerchief to shreds and smashed up the furniture. Felicia cowered in a corner.

The next day Othello brought her a chest of jewels by way of apology. Felicia ran her fingers through them, letting the rubies, sapphires, emeralds, and diamonds fall like sparkling rain.

"Don't you like them?" her husband asked.

"They're nice," Felicia said listlessly.

"What would please you, my little partridge? A new dress? A pony? Perfume?"

"I'm lonely," Felicia admitted. "I miss the pleasant conversations of my mother and sister. When you're gone I have no one to talk to."

"Nothing could be simpler to fix," cried Lord Othello. "As it happens, I'm going away for a month tomorrow and

I'll invite Anne to keep you company." He sent a messenger at once.

Felicia and Anne fell into each other's arms. They ran from room to room, with Felicia proudly showing off the gifts Othello had given her. She was gripped by a kind of fever after so many days without conversation.

Othello smiled indulgently. "Dear wife," he said, "I am of course devastated at leaving you again, but I wish you to enjoy yourself during my absence. Here are the keys to all my worldly goods. This one opens the room where I keep gold and silver. This is for jewels and this for sweetmeats, candied rose petals, and so forth. But there is one door you may not enter at the back of the garden. If you dare to open that, doom shall fall upon you like a lightning bolt from heaven. It's this little key here. See? The one engraved with a rose."

"Forgive me, Lord Othello," said Anne, "but why give Felicia a key she may not use?"

"Why not, since I trust her completely?" the Moor replied. He mounted his great black stallion and set off on his journey. The gate was bolted and locked behind him.

"He took *that* key with him, you notice," said Anne. "We are trapped here until he returns."

But Felicia wasn't concerned. She was far more interested in exploring the rooms she had not yet seen. They opened door after door and discovered many treasures, including a library. Anne could read, and Felicia enjoyed listening. Several pleasant days passed with neither of them suffering from boredom.

"Look here," said Anne one day. "This book was written by Othello himself. It's about his travels in North Africa and—oh, see!—about his life in Rome, Genoa, Milan, Pisa, Naples, and Venice. In Rome he says he married someone called Lydia. In Genoa he wed Lucinda."

Anne took the book into the garden where the light was better. She read as rapidly as she could, but there was so much information it took a long time. "There's someone named Flora in Milan, Maria in Pisa, Sophia in Naples and—and—in Venice he married Desdemona!"

"Many women die in childbed," Felicia faltered.

"Not her! That was the rumor I heard in the marketplace," cried Anne. "Othello *strangled* Desdemona. It was a terrific scandal and he had to flee."

"Are you sure?" said Felicia, turning pale.

"Of course I'm sure! I was right all along! The forbidden door conceals the bodies of his dead wives," Anne said fiercely. "We have to get out of here. Fortunately, I have made a plan."

They climbed to the tallest tower of the castle, carrying the mirror with them. Anne stood on a chair next to the window. She could see the Trephine mansion on the other side of the valley, its rose-colored walls contrasting nicely with dark green cypresses. "Now I'm going to lean outside," Anne said. "Don't distract me, because this mirror is heavy."

She held the mirror up to catch the sun. A bright spot of light flashed across the valley and landed on the balcony of the Trephine mansion. "Whew!" said Anne, sliding to the floor. "That's hard work. I'll need to rest before I try again."

"But what are you doing?" said Felicia.

"I told Mother before I left that if she saw a flash of light, she was to send Arturo, Rodrigo, Fidelio, and Giovanni to rescue us. I hope she's watching. It would be like her to have gone visiting." Again and again Anne leaned out the window with the heavy mirror.

Felicia sat below. Every five minutes she said, "Anne, sister Anne, do you see anyone coming?" It was like a child whining *are we there yet?* on a long trip.

"Stop bothering me!" cried Anne at last, and the mirror slipped out of her hands and crashed down onto the flagstones below. "Well, that's done it," panted Anne, coming back inside. "I have no idea whether our message was received."

"Anne, sister Anne—" began Felicia.

"If you say that one more time, I'm going to break a chair over your head."

They waited, watching anxiously for a plume of dust that would indicate the arrival of their brothers. For a long time nothing happened, and then Anne spotted something. "I think they're coming—oh, pooh! It's only a flock of sheep."

Anne stayed bravely at her post, and after a while she saw another cloud of dust. "It's got to be them this time," she said, but it was only a group of peddlers making their way to market.

"Third time lucky," said Anne, shading her eyes to observe the bright road. And the third time they *were* lucky, for Arturo, Rodrigo, Fidelio, and Giovanni were galloping at top speed toward the castle along with all their men. They arrived with iron bars and pried the gate open.

They really enjoyed doing things like that. It was almost as much fun as hunting. "What's the matter? Why do you need rescuing?" cried Arturo, brandishing his sword.

"Othello has murdered his former wives and hidden their bodies behind that door," said Anne, producing the little key engraved with the rose. She unlocked it. Her brothers and their followers crowded through—

On the other side was the most charming garden imaginable. A fountain splashed. Orange and almond trees offered welcome shade. In fact, it was an exact copy of the garden in front, and around it were as many rooms. In the middle sat Lord Othello, surrounded by a bevy of beautiful women in gauze pantaloons and little sequined blouses. At least a dozen children scattered at the sight of the soldiers.

Othello rose and bowed to the intruders. "I had expected Felicia to be overcome with curiosity and open the door. All my other wives did. But you are welcome in spite of the rude entrance you made. May I introduce Fatima, Gertrude, Ludmilla, Hortense, Lydia, Lucinda, Flora, Maria, Sophia, and Desdemona?"

"You . . . *didn't* murder them?" Anne said faintly.

"What kind of monster do you think I am? You see," said the Moorish prince, "my religion allows me more than one of these treasures. Leo understood that, but the Inquisitors, curse them, wanted me to divorce all but one. Where's the justice in that? Which of these adored creatures could I abandon? And so I had to move every time they were discovered. I must say, I'm getting tired of pulling up stakes."

"Well, you aren't taking our sister," declared Arturo.

"I always give my wives a choice when they discover the harem," Othello said. "Felicia, my little dumpling, wouldn't you like to see Paris? They have wonderful dressmakers, and you wouldn't be lonely with the other ladies around." But Felicia only hid her face and wept.

"We must preserve her reputation," Anne said firmly.

"Oh, very well! You may spread the usual rumors," Othello said. "Felicia may keep the castle and one of the chests of gold."

Felicia returned to her mother's house until the current inhabitants of the castle could depart. Anne made up the story of Bluebeard, and very popular it was, too. It made her sister an instant celebrity. Noblemen came from all over to see the place where Bluebeard was slain, and of course they stayed behind to admire the two brave sisters.

Late one evening, a caravan camped in a forest next to a river. "I'm going to love Paris," said Lord Othello, surrounded by his adoring wives and children. "The French have absolutely wonderful food, art, music, literature, and women." The Moor looked around at his flock and his diminishing resources. "Perhaps not women," he decided.

So they all moved into a chateau overlooking the Seine and lived happily ever after. And Othello never took another wife.

Nancy Farmer is the author of *The House of the Scorpion*; *The Ear, the Eye and the Arm*; and *A Girl Named Disaster*. She had a mother who not only read her fairy tales but actually believed that fairies lived in the garden. Her father was forbidden to cut down trees because the tree spirits would cry. In such a setting, naturally, reality was tenuous.

Nancy chose Bluebeard because he seemed the most difficult villain to rehabilitate. But to her delight she discovered an actual historical precedent. The character of Othello was based on a real Moroccan nobleman enslaved by the most venal and rascally Pope Leo X. The lesson here, O readers, is that fairy tales and history share the same bedroom and, like devoted sisters, borrow each other's clothes.

'Skin
Michael Cadnum

1

I have but one wicked habit, and this I think can be forgiven, in light of my many graces.

Let's set aside any recounting of what makes me undesirable. Let's discuss my virtues. They abound. For a first example of my gifts to humankind: the bridge. What passed for bridges always collapsed until I created improvements. I invented the bridge as it became known throughout the kingdom.

I invented many other boons to humankind, as well. Bread was always flat as crackers until I taught bakers to breed yeast, and meat was always chewed raw until I whispered in the ear of the king's top chef and encouraged him to experiment with roasting.

I created so much of what makes life enjoyable. Buckles? I smithed the first set, and left them on the harness-maker's bench to be discovered the next dawn. The yoke?

That was me, tired of seeing oxen stumble together or try to wander in opposite directions, tipping nourishing loads of harvest into the mud.

It was easy to find where my talents were required. The kingdom was blessed—if that is the right word—with a breed of talkative jackdaw, a bird like a gray crow with a sooty head. These jackdaws would wing by, chattering and singing of the brewer's sour beer, or the maiden's unbroken fever, and I would hurry off to help or cure, as the case warranted.

I breathed metaphors into the nodding poet's ear. I waxed wise, and encouraged the tipsy parson to dip his pen and round out his sermon with a sober blessing. I was a busy sprite, and I was happy to be of unrewarded service to mankind.

I created these blessings in secret, unseen, unthanked, with a whisper and a quick touch while the clockmaker or the shipwright was not looking. But some need had begun to simmer in me once again, some longing that my own generosity could not meet.

And what, one might wonder, was the slight, pernicious habit that blemished my otherwise purely beneficent character?

To be brief, I kill and eat human babies.

2

The particular splendid morning when my future was altered entirely I was busy contriving, by nudge and murmur, to get window-makers to make glass.

They would never have imagined such a substance without my help. It was tricky work involving heat and judgment. Just as sand was melting into a fluid, word arrived that the miller's daughter was imprisoned in the king's tower.

"King Charles the Wise has locked up Winnie," said the town crier. "All so she can spin straw into gold, as her father bragged she could." He added, his eyes bright with curiosity, "Tell me what you're doing."

"We're busy melting sand and getting ready to manufacture—" The window-maker paused.

I whispered into his ear, invisible and intense. Such a whisper sounds to the bemused recipient like the murmur of his own faculties.

"We're producing glass," concluded the master window-maker with a confident smile. "Glass is what we're making, and great panes of the stuff, too. Best not get too close—it's hot."

I had admired Winnie, the miller's daughter, for some time, all without her knowing it. Hearing of her imprisonment, I was both vexed and grieved, believing that certainly a woman of beautiful form will have an equally pleasing disposition.

I winked my way through the bright air and appeared before the sobbing lass, deep in the smallest chamber of the king's stone tower.

"Why the tears, dear Winnie?" I inquired.

She did not hear me, weeping and cursing her father's boastful foolishness. "Greetings, Winnie, dear lass," I tried once more. "Allow me to help."

It was difficult for me to stand still enough to allow a human being to take in the sight of me, but I made the effort, stilling my normally effervescent limbs and doing all but holding my breath so she might behold me as I stood there, surrounded by great, fragrant heaps of freshly scythed straw.

She dabbed her tears with the lace cuff of her sleeve, and then her eyes grew round. She stared. She took a breath of air and stared some more, right at me.

"You wizened little imp," she exclaimed, "what possible use are you?"

"My dear young Winnie," I replied, "I can spin this straw into as much gold as any practical monarch might desire."

"For what in exchange, you little weevil?" she asked, with a certain bluntness.

"For your thanks," I said, and I set to work.

The spinning wheel was a contrivance of my own devising—before I came along, the kingdom dressed in hare skins and dried and woven reeds. A pleasant sound it made, my singing wheel, as straw spun into sweeps of golden wire, cascades spiraling in the slits of sunlight that woke the world the next dawn.

Not that the spinning was easy. Magic this was not, so much as labor—elfin work, but effort nevertheless. She woke from her sleep as I slumped wearily beside the wheel. "Oh, thanks," she said with a yawn.

3

King Charles the Wise clapped his hands.

"Well, done, Winnie!" exclaimed the royal voice. "Do this again tonight and I'll have a pretty prize for you indeed."

Winnie dimpled and blushed. "My lord king," she said, "just making all this rich metal for you is prize enough for me."

Winnie was set into a larger cell, with all the more straw, but she waited half bored while I offered my reassurance, telling her never to worry.

"I'm not worried," she said.

I prepared once more to spin these bushels of straw, still moist from the field and inhabited by startled ladybirds and struggling butterflies, which I managed to rescue. I transformed the amber stalks of harvest into the heavy, supple element humans prize as treasure.

I admire gold well enough, although I think that a stem

of straw is as splendid as any precious metal mined from the underworld. And I was aware as I labored, sweatily churning out orbits of twenty-four-karat wealth, that Winnie was overcome with ennui, sleeping, waking, and asking from time to time, "Aren't you done yet?"

My efforts drained the power from my limbs and sapped my ability to speak. "Thanks," she said after the wearisome night had passed and I was done. And I staggered to the corner of the chamber and made myself invisible.

"Winnie, you are a treasure," said King Charles, all smiles. He is a tall, well-favored man with a ruddy face and auburn beard. "I am astonished and grateful." He fingered a loop of the great accordions of spun gold. "If you—or whatever magic sustains you—can accomplish this marvel for one more night, I shall give you the most wonderful reward in the kingdom."

"And what, my lord king," asked Winnie, with a blushing smile, "could that be?"

"Me!" the king said with a laugh. "You shall be my queen!"

It was another night of long and numbing labor for me. This latest delivery of straw was too fresh, still green and moist with summer rain. Sparrows had been gathered in the harvesters' haste, and I helped more than one to the window slits and out into the night air.

"Hurry up," said Winnie.

I could not go on spinning stem and chaff into treasure. My arms ached, my head pounded with a persistent pain that caused my vision to flicker and grow faint. "Do your work, you little wood-rat," said Winnie, "or I'll have the guard in to twist your neck."

I considered her threat. I began to realize that I did not enjoy her company as much as I once had.

"I'll finish this work, Winnie," I said, "if you promise me that I can come and visit you when you have children."

"You want to eat my babies, I suspect," said Winnie, not appalled so much as fascinated, in a bored sort of way.

I was shocked at her coarseness. "I want to enjoy them."

"Enjoy them in a pudding, most likely, I'll wager," said Winnie. "I've heard stories about elves like you."

"I'll not spin another splinter into gold," I said, folding my arms, "unless you agree."

She gave an airy wave. "Sure, come visit us, strange little creature, what do I care, as long as you complete your task? The king's guards will put you in chains as soon as look at you."

I heard the tidings many months later, thanks to the vocal jackdaws, all about the wedding feast, and at length, a new little baby was born to the royal couple. "It's a girl!" echoed the talkative birds, with, I believe, some joy in their tidings.

I was occupied with the creation of silk, inspiring the planting of mulberry trees and the collection of cocoons, and I was also involved in the invention of the compass, a wondrous aid to sailors and explorers alike, sure to save lives. I had little time for Queen Winifred and her king.

But the day came when my hidden nature got the best of me. Giving mankind useful inventions and valuable hints did not satisfy my deep hunger for a ripe and dimpled baby princess to eat.

In a word, I was hungry.

Hungry does not describe my appetite. I was famished. I was ravenous. Nothing would satisfy this growing craving but a feast of royal baby.

I whisked my way to the playroom of the infant princess, delighted to see her ruddy little countenance, safe and sleeping in her nurse's arms. I was so seized by hunger for the baby Elizabeth, as she had been christened, that I forgot myself and stood entirely rapt and still, with no attempt to hide or hurry.

"You scoundrel," came a cry. "You devious, infant-stealing little devil!"

It was Queen Winnie, her eyes alight with protective-ness and anger, and it was this last characterization of me that stung the worst. A devil I am not, not by habit or inclination.

But I was quite famished for a particular delicacy. "If you do not guess my name this hour tomorrow," I said, in my best, most high-elfin accent, "I shall take this infant away with me to a life of mercy and marvel."

"Sirrah," she retorted, "I shall guess your name with the help of the loyal jackdaws of my husband's realm. Now leave this place, or I'll call the royal guard and they'll chop you into pieces."

4

I went home to the woodland and opened my coffer of treasures and dusted off my cookbooks.

A casserole would not be grand enough, I decided. I would roast the little princess, baste her with butter and mustard, sprinkle her with rosemary, garnish her flesh with garlic cloves. I was getting hungrier and hungrier, anticipating my forthcoming meal.

In the end I decided that I would not bother with gar-nish and sauces, or with hot coals and the nuisance of the iron spit and the steel knife. When I got my hands on the ripe, wee Elizabeth, I would have baby-in-arms sushi, infant done rare, so rare as to be still alive. I would eat her right then and there!

I noticed the jackdaws fluttering in the oak trees overhead as I put away my heirloom recipes.

"Well," I exclaimed in a stage whisper, "Queen Winnie will never come close to guessing that my name is—"

I paused, and came up with an outlandish appellation, one no elf would ever possess. "The queen will never guess that my name is the round and splendid *Rumplestiltskin!*"

Jackdaws, you noisy, handsome birds. I saw you winging, in your enthusiastic way, back toward the castle, and I knew that you carried the secret of my altogether fictitious name. I could hear the raucous imitation, *Rumplestiltskin, Rumplestiltskin,* on the evening air.

Queen Winnie rattled off "Rumplestiltskin!" as soon as she set eyes on me at court the next morning.

She stood up and pointed. She laughed—she jeered!

I gave a quiet laugh.

"My dear Queen Winnie, the jackdaws have deceived you, just as I intended. I bear no such silly name, and I shall take little Elizabeth right now, if you please."

I seized the swaddled infant from the nurse's arms, and I ate her.

I shoved her whole, head first, into my mouth, and—

barely chewing—I inhaled the length and breadth of her little body in one great gulp. And I laughed. I celebrated my victory and my quickly finished feast. I cavorted in happiness at first, but then in growing horror. The realization seized me that something was amiss with my gobbled supper.

I gagged.

I staggered, fell, and writhed. I retched—but forgive me. In my anguish at remembering the details of that catastrophe, I may trespass on good taste.

Charles the Wise had not earned his name by being dull. He had prepared a backup scheme, in fear that the jackdaws' reports, though earnest, might prove to be in error. He prepared a baby of wax and chalk, mixed with elf-bane and spider venom, and caused the Queen's ladies of the wardrobe to powder and paint the puppet into the semblance of a drowsing babe.

I lay down upon the polished stone floor of the royal court, and—in all but the most literal sense of the word—I died.

The gentle, reddish-bearded monarch leaned over me and picked me up by the legs. He shook and slapped me until my dinner coughed up out of me, nearly as whole as I had seen it last.

"Cage the sprite," said the farseeing king to his approaching guards. "But hurt him not, whatever his name might be."

5

The button? I devised it.

The magnifying glass? That's mine, too.

And more—much more. I served the king and his kingdom from a cage in a cell in a tower. I lived on cheese, like a farmer. The king visited with me, and I gave him my most recent offering: sea charts, perfume, the lute. I supped on goat's curd and survived on whey.

Deadbolt, padlock, combination catch. I invented them all. I devised the chute, the elastic cord, the glider, the underground passage.

The king is grateful.

"We are so lucky to have you, What's-Your-Name," he laughs.

You may wonder what is my true name, after all?

Someday soon you will be able to call me Laughs-at-Chains, as I slip through your village to dine.

Michael Cadnum's thirty-second book, *Peril on the Sea*, tells the true story of the attack by the Spanish Armada, and his recent novel, *The King's Arrow*, tells the true story of the mysterious death of King William II of England. Michael Cadnum writes poetry as well as fiction, and loves to go for long walks in the San Francisco Bay Area, where he lives. His writing has won many awards.

Michael says, regarding the character Rumplestiltskin: "The wonderful tale of this powerful elf is about the power of naming—if you know the name of something you have command over it. And if you think about it, this is true, because to name something accurately, whether you are considering a disease, a rare mineral, or a person, you have to know something about it.

"But I always felt there was more to the legend than that—or there should have been. If an elf could spin straw into gold, couldn't he do other things just as well? I loved working on this story, and I believed I have discovered that the answer to this question is an emphatic *yes*."

A Delicate Architecture

Catherynne M. Valente

My father was a confectioner. I slept on pillows of spun sugar; when I woke, the sweat and tears of my dreams had melted it all to nothing, and my cheek rested on the crisp sheets of red linen. Many things in my father's house were made of candy, for he was a prodigy, having at the age of five invented a chocolate trifle so dark and rich that the new emperor's chocolatier sat down upon the steps of his great golden kitchen and wept into his truffle-dusted mustache. So it was that when my father found himself in possession of a daughter, he cut her corners and measured her sweetness with no less precision than he used in his candies.

My breakfast plate was clear, hard butterscotch, full of oven bubbles. I ate my soft-boiled marzipan egg gingerly, tapping its little cap with a toffee hammer. The yolk within was a lemony syrup that dribbled out into my eggcup. I drank chocolate from a black vanilla-bean mug. But I ate sugared plums with a fork of sparrow bones; the marrow left salt in the fruit, and the strange, thick taste of a thing once alive in all that sugar. When I asked my father why I should taste these bones along with the sweetness of the candied plums, he told me very seriously that I must always remember that sugar was once alive. It grew tall and green and hard as my own knuckles in a faraway place, under a red sun that burned on the face of the sea. I must always remember that children just like me cut it down and crushed it up with tan and strong hands, and that their sweat, which gave me my sugar, tasted also of salt.

"If you forget that red sun and those long, green stalks, then you are not truly a confectioner. You understand nothing about candy but that it tastes good and is colorful—and these things a pig can tell, too. We are the angels of the cane, we are oven magicians, but if you would rather be a pig snuffling in the leaves . . ."

"No, Papa."

"Well then, eat your plums, magician of my heart."

And so I did, and the tang of marrow in the sugar-meat was rich and disturbing and sweet.

Often I would ask my father where my mother had gone, if she had not liked her fork of sparrow bones, or if she had not wanted to eat marzipan eggs every day. These were the only complaints I could think of. My father ruffled my hair with his sticky hand and said:

"One morning, fine as milk, when I lived in Vienna and reclined on turquoise cushions, with the empress licking my fingers for one taste of my sweets, I went walking past the city shops, my golden cane cracking on the cobbles, peering into their frosted windows and listening to the silver bells strung from the doors. In the window of a competitor who hardly deserved the name, being but a poor maker of trifles which would hardly satisfy a duchess, I saw the loveliest little crystal jar. It was as intricately cut as a diamond and full of the purest sugar I have ever seen. The little shopkeeper, bent with decades of hunching over trays of chocolate, smiled at me with few enough teeth and cried:

"'Alonzo! I see you have cast your discerning gaze upon my little vial of sugar! I assure you it is the finest of all the sugars ever made, rendered from the tallest cane in the isles by a fortunate virgin snatched at the last moment from the frothing red mouth of her volcano! It was then blanched to the snowy shade you see in a bath of lion's milk and ground to sweetest dust with a pearl pestle, and finally poured into a jar made from the glass of three church windows. I am no emperor's darling, but in this I exceed you at last!'

"The little man did a shambling dance of joy, to my

disgust. But I poured out coins onto his scale until his eyes gleamed wet with longing, and took that little jar away with me."

My father pinched my chin affectionately. "I hurried back home, boiled the sugar with costly dyes and other secret things, and poured it into a Constanze-shaped mold, slid it into the oven, and out you came in an hour or two, eyes shining like caramels!"

My father laughed when I pulled his ear and told him not to tease me, that every girl has a mother, and an oven is no proper mother! He gave me a slice of honeycomb and shooed me into the garden, where raspberries grew along the white gate.

And thus I grew up. I ate my egg every morning and licked the yolk from my lips. I ate my plums with my bone fork and thought very carefully about the tall cane under the red sun. I scrubbed my pillow from my cheeks until they were quite pink. Every old woman in the village remarked on how much I resembled the little ivory cameos of the empress, the same delicate nose, high brow, thick red hair. I begged my father to let me go to Vienna, as he had done when he was a boy. After all, I was far from a dense child. I had my suspicions—I wanted to see the empress.

I wanted to hear the violas playing in white halls with

green-and-rose-checkered floors. I wanted to ride a horse with long brown reins. I wanted to taste radishes and carrots and potatoes, even a chicken, even a fish on a plate of real porcelain, with no oven bubbles in it.

"Why did we leave Vienna, Papa?" I cried, over our supper of marshmallow crèmes and caramel cakes. "I could have learned to play the flute there; I could have worn a wig like spun sugar. You learned these things—why may I not?"

My father's face reddened and darkened all at once, and he gripped the sides of the butcher's board where he cut caramel into bricks. "I learned to prefer sugar to white curls," he growled, "and peppermints to piccolos, and cherry creams to the empress. You will learn this, too, Constanze." He cleared his throat. "It is an important thing to know."

I bent myself to the lesson. I learned how to test my father's syrups by dropping them into silver pots of cold water. By the time I was sixteen, I hardly needed to do it; I could sense the hard crack of finished candy, feel the brittle snap prickling the hairs of my neck. My fingers were red with so· many crushed berries; my palms were dry and crackling with the pale and scratchy wrapping papers we used for penny sweets. I was a good girl. By the time my father gave me the dress, I was a better confectioner than he, though he would never admit it. It was almost like magic, the way candies would form, glistening and impossibly colorful, under my hands.

It was very bright that morning. The light came through the windowpanes like butterscotch plates. When I came into the kitchen, there was no egg on the table, no toffee hammer, no chocolate in a sweet black cup. Instead, lying over the cold oven, like a cake waiting to be iced, was a dress. It was the color of ink, tiered and layered like the ones Viennese ladies wore in my dreams, floating blue to the floor, dusted with diamonds that caught the morning light and flashed cheerfully.

"Oh, Papa! Where would I wear a thing like that?"

My father smiled broadly, but the corners of his smile were wilted and sad.

"Vienna," he said. "The court. I thought you wanted to go, to wear a wig, to hear a flute?"

He helped me on with the dress, and as he cinched in my waist and lifted my red hair from bare shoulders, I realized that the dress was made of hard blue sugar and thousands of blueberry skins stitched together with syrupy thread. The diamonds were lumps of crystal candy, still a bit sticky, and at the waist were icing flowers in a white cascade. Nothing of that dress was not sweet, was not sugar, was not my father's trade and mine.

Vienna looked like a Christmas cake we had once made for a baroness: all hard, white curls and creases and carvings, like someone had draped the city in vanilla cream. There were brown horses, and brown carriages attached to them. In the emperor's palace, where my father walked as though he had built it, there were green-and-rose-checkered floors, and violas playing somewhere far off. My father took my hand and led me to a room which was harder and whiter than all the rest, where the emperor and the empress sat frowning on terrible silver thrones of sharpened filigree, like two demons on their wedding day. I gasped, and shrank behind my father, the indigo train of my dress showing dark against the floor. I could not hope to hide from those awful royal eyes.

"Why have you brought us this thing, Alonzo?" barked the emperor, who had a short blond mustache and copper buttons running down his chest. "This thing which bears such a resemblance to our wife? Do you insult us by dragging this reminder of your crimes and hers across our floor like a dust broom?"

The empress blushed deeply, her skin going the same shade as her hair, the same shade as my hair. My father clenched his teeth.

"I told you then, when you loved my chocolates above

all things, that I did not touch her, that I loved her as a man loves God, not as he loves a woman."

"Yet you come back, begging to return to my grace, towing a child who is a mirror of her! This is obscene, Alonzo!"

My father's face broke open, pleading. It was terrible to see him so. I clutched my icing flowers, confused and frightened.

"But she is not my child! She is not the empress's child! She is the greatest thing I have ever created, the greatest of all things I have baked in my oven. I have brought her to show you what I may do in your name, for your grace, if you will look on me with love again, if you will give me your favor once more. If you will let me come back to the city, to my home."

I gaped, and tears filled my eyes. My father drew a little silver icing spade from his belt and started toward me. I cried out and my voice echoed in the hard, white hall like a sparrow cut into a fork. I cringed, but my father gripped my arms tight as a tureen's handles, and his eyes were wide and wet. He pushed me to my knees on the emperor's polished floor, and the two monarchs watched impassively as I wept in my beautiful blue dress, though the empress let a pale hand flutter to her throat. My father put the spade to my neck and scraped it up, across my skin, like a barber giving a young man his first shave.

A shower of sugar fell glittering across my chest.

"I never lied to you, Constanze," he murmured in my ear.

He pierced my cheek with the tip of the spade, and blood trickled down my chin, over my lips. It tasted like raspberries.

"Look at her, your majesty. She is nothing but sugar, nothing but candy, through and through. I made her in my own oven. I raised her up. Now she is grown—and so beautiful! Look at her cinnamon hair, her marzipan skin, her tears of sugar and salt! And you may have her, you may have the greatest confection made on this earth, if you will but let me come home, and make you chocolates as I used to, and put your hand to my shoulder in friend-ship again."

The empress rose from her throne and walked toward me, like a mirror gliding on a hidden track, so like me she was, though her gown was golden, and its train lon-ger than the hall. She looked at me, her gaze pointed and deep, but did not seem to hear my sobbing or see my tears. She put her hand to my bleeding cheek and tasted the blood on her palm, daintily, with the tip of her tongue.

"She looks so much like me, Alonzo. It is a strange thing to see."

My father flushed. "I was lonely," he whispered. "And

perhaps a man may be forgiven for casting a doll's face in the image of God."

I was kept in the kitchens, hung up on the wall like a copper pot or a length of garlic. Every day a cook would clip my fingernails to sweeten the emperor's coffee, or cut off a curl of my scarlet hair to spice the Easter cakes of the empress's first child—a boy with brown eyes like my father's. Sometimes the head cook would lance my cheek carefully and collect the scarlet syrup in a hard white cup. Once they plucked my eyelashes, ever so gently, for a licorice comfit the empress's new daughter craved. They were kind enough to ice my lids between plucking.

They tried not to cause me any pain. Cooks and confectioners are not wicked creatures by nature, and the younger kitchen girls were disturbed by the shape of me hanging there, toes pointed at the oven. Eventually, they grew accustomed to it, and I was no more strange to them than a shaker of salt or a pepper mill. My dress sagged and browned, as blueberry skins will do, and fell away. A kind little boy who scrubbed the floors brought me a coarse black dress from his mother's closet. It was made of wool, real wool, from a sheep and not an oven. They fed me radishes and carrots and potatoes, and sometimes chicken, sometimes even fish, on a plate of real porcelain, with no heat bubbles in it, none at all.

I grew old on that wall, my marzipan skin withered and wrinkled no less than flesh, helped along by lancings and scrapings and trimmings. My hair turned white and fell out, eagerly collected. As I grew old, I was told that the emperor liked the taste of my hair better and better, and soon I was bald.

But emperors die, and so do fathers. Both of these occurred in their way, and when at last the empress died, there was no one to remember that the source of the palace sugar was not a far-off isle under a red sun that burned on the face of the sea. On the wall, I thought of that red sun often, and the children cutting cane, and the taste of the bird's marrow deep in my plum. That same kind floor-scrubber, grown up and promoted to butler, cut me down when my bones were brittle and touched my shorn hair gently. But he did not apologize. How could he? How many cakes and teas had he tasted which were sweetened by me?

I ran from the palace in the night, as much as I could run, an old, scraped-out crone, a witch in a black dress stumbling across the city and through, across and out. I kept running and running, my sugar body burning and shrieking with disuse. I ran past the hard white streets and past the villages where I had been a child who knew nothing of Vienna, into the woods, into the black forest with the creeping loam and nothing sweet for miles. Only there did I stop, panting, my spiced breath fogging in the air. There were great dark green boughs arching over me, pine and larch and oak. I sank down to the earth, wrung dry of weeping, safe and far from anything hard, anything white, anything with accusing eyes on a throne like a demon's wedding. No one would scrape me for teatime again. No one would touch me again. I put my hands to my head and stared up at the stars through the leaves. It was quiet, at last—quiet, and dark. I curled up on the leaves and slept.

When I woke, I was cold. I shivered. I needed more than a black dress to cover me. I would not go back, not to any place which had known me, not to Vienna, not to a village without a candy-maker. I would not hang a sign over a door and feed sweets to children. I would stay in the dark, under the green. And so I needed a house. But I knew nothing of houses. I was not a bricklayer or a thatcher. I did not know how to make a chimney. I did not know how to make a door hinge. I did not know how to stitch curtains.

But I knew how to make candy.

I went begging in the villages, a harmless old crone—

was it odd that she asked for sugar and not for coins? Certainly. Did they think it mad that she begged for berries and liquors and cocoa, but never alms? Of course. But the elderly are strange and their ways inexplicable to the young. I collected, just as they had done from me all my years on the wall, and my hair grew. I went to my place in the forest, under the black and the boughs, and I poured a foundation of caramel. I raised up thick, brown gingerbread walls, with cinnamon for wattle and marshmallow for daub. Hard-crack windows clear as the morning air, a smoking licorice chimney, stairs of peanut brittle and carpets of red taffy, a peppermint bathtub. And a great black oven, all of blackened, burnt sugar, with a yellow flame within. Gumdrops studded my house like jewels, and a little path of molasses ran liquid and dark from my door. And when my hair had grown long enough, I thatched my roof with cinnamon strands.

It had such a delicate architecture, my house that I baked and built. It was as delicately made as I had been. I thought of my father all the while, and the red sun on waving green cane. I thought of him while I built my pastry table, and I thought of him while I built my gingerbread floors. I hated and loved him in turns, as witches will do, for our hearts are strange and inexplicable. He had never come to see me on the wall, even once. I could not understand it. But I made my caramel bricks, and I rolled out sheets of toffee onto my bed, and I told his ghost that I was a good girl, I had always been a good girl, even on the wall.

I made a pillow of spun sugar. I made plates of butterscotch. Each morning I tapped a marzipan egg with a little toffee hammer. But I never caught a sparrow for my plums. They are so very quick. I was always hungry for them, for something living and salty and sweet amid all my sugar. I longed for something alive in my crystalline house, something to remind me of the children crushing up cane with tan, strong hands. There was no marrow in my plums. I could not remember the red sun and the long, green stalks, and so I bent low in my lollipop rocking chair, weeping and whispering to my father that I was sorry, I was sorry, I was no more than a pig snuffling in the leaves after all.

And one morning, when it was very bright, and the light came through the window like a viola playing something very sweet and sad, I heard footsteps coming up my molasses path. Children: a boy and a girl. They laughed, and over their heads blackbirds cawed hungrily.

I was hungry, too.

Catherynne M. Valente, born in the Pacific Northwest, is the author of the Orphan's Tales series, as well as *The Labyrinth*, *Yume no Hon: The Book of Dreams*, *The Grass-Cutting Sword*, and four books of poetry. She currently lives in Maine with her two dogs.

Catherynne says: "'Hansel and Gretel' has always been one of my favorite fairy tales. The image of the candy house is so compelling and surreal. This is my second retelling of it—the first was from Gretel's point of view—and I wanted to know what kind of person would end up in such a house. Why would she build it that way? Where did she come from? Why is she so obsessed with food and eating? The academic answers never satisfied me. I know intellectually that women are associated with food in folklore, and bad women with cannibalism, and that children are drawn to candy, so that the house is a perfect lure, but that didn't satisfy me at a gut level. I wanted to know the witch's name. I wanted to know why she wants to eat a child. I chose to open up the beginning of this tale, and to end with the beginning of the traditional one, so that the witch who lived in the gingerbread house would have a history, a life, a name."

Molly

Midori Snyder

The townhouse had been beautiful once long ago in the past, when the cantaloupe-colored walls were fresh. Swags of carved ivy adorned the lintels of the roof, and among the curling leaves, sculpted cupids smiled down at the well-dressed people in the street. In the winter, women wore hats with plumes of white ostrich feathers. Their coats were trimmed with fox fur, and they tucked their delicate hands into muffs of silk-lined mink. Men wore bowlers and gabardine greatcoats with a touch of velvet on the collar. In the summer there were nannies in starched aprons pushing babies in sailor suits down the street in plush prams. There were carriages with sleek horses, and doormen with white gloves. Roses tumbled over the gates, and small dogs at the end of expensive leashes peed against the iron fences.

But over time, what was grand faded, what was rich became poor, and what was lovely became mean. Rain and sun blasted the bright face of the townhouse until the paint flaked and peeled like a rind. The cupids lost their smiles, the ivy leaves were chipped, and the wealthy men and women moved to bigger mansions with a view of the river or the woods. Gaunt horses plodded up the street dragging junk wagons. Families piled into the lovely apartments in threes and fours and fives, like storm-tossed survivors setting camp in every available space. Women hung the washing between the windows, and patched broken panes with butcher paper. Husbands weary from long hours in nearby factories staggered home from taverns, and equally weary wives cursed them for their lack of coins. Children wearing last year's shoes and hand-me-down clothes too big or too small scrambled up and down the hallways, screaming and shouting.

On the top floor of the townhouse lived one family, the Dongoggles, who were different from the rest. They had lived there a long time, so long no one knew for sure when they had moved into the building. They were odd, maybe even aloof. Missus Dongoggle was never seen hanging her washing out the window, never heard screaming at her husband. Laundry women came and carried away armloads of petticoats and sheets only to return them a day latter freshly laundered. The grocer brought bottles of wine and baskets of vegetables and cheeses. The butcher's boy came, staggering under the weight of meat wrapped in white paper packages and tied with string. The women of the townhouse noticed such things and pursed their lips as if sucking lemons. Mr. Dongoggle walked out every morning in a suit of good cloth, and he returned every evening as fresh as he had left. The men noticed such things, and they shoved their shoulders hard into their neighbors until they swore. The three Dongoggle girls, each alike in every way, wore striped pinafores, new stockings, and polished shoes. They carried teddy bears and sweets. The children noticed such things and burst into uncontrollable tears on the rare days when the girls left the top floor and walked down the street.

But one child did not cry. She did not suck her sour lips or beat her fists into the closest little child. She watched and schemed. And she knew something about the Dongoggles was not quite right.

"Molly, git yerself in here girl before I thrash the lights out of you," screamed the Missus Whuppie. "There's mending to be done, and I'll take the spoon to ye if you don't git a move on."

"Coming, Ma," Molly answered, her eyes narrowing on the figure of Mr. Dongoggle in his pinstriped suit slowly taking the stairs, one heavy foot at a time. She waited on the landing, squatting down so as to have a good long look in his face as he ascended toward her floor. A few more steps and there he was, eye-level. He was a brute of a man, gray skinned and heavy jawed beneath the bowler. His amber eyes bulged, barely shaded by thin lids. His mushroomed nose quivered when he saw her, and a thick red tongue touched his lips. He stopped, furred brow pulled in question. Molly peered closely at his mottled skin, the jagged line of teeth that snagged on his upper lip. She caught the scent of musk mingled with the sickly sweet odor of peppermint. She glanced at his eyes and saw the threads of darker brown that spun away from a diamond-shaped iris. The thin lids snapped shut, but not before she had seen something.

Oh yes, she thought. *You've a secret, don't you? And won't I be the girl to ferret it out. And won't you be paying me the little coins to keep it quiet. Not from here, are ye? Oh no,* she decided, *no right to take what's ours, what's mine.*

She leaned back against the door, her mother still calling for her, and smiled smugly at the large man continuing up the stairs.

"That one knows, Irene," Mr. Dongoggle said as he and Missus Dongoggle lay that night in their huge bed, heads propped up against thunderclouds of goose-down pillows.

"Nonsense," Irene answered. "You don't know human

children. They've very little imagination when it comes to adults." She tucked the stray ends of her long braid into her nightcap.

"*Human* adults," Dongoggle replied. "But there have been ones before that have hurt, even killed, our kind. I think we should leave. Perhaps it's time to go home."

"But we *are* home," Irene said forcefully. She was a slender woman, with a pointed chin and large gray eyes. Next to her husband she looked small as a child, except for her hands. Lying on the coverlet they were uncommonly broad, the fingers rough and callused.

"I miss the forest," he sighed.

"I do not," she said tartly. "And neither do the girls. They like it here. They like wearing dresses and reading books. And they are making friends."

Dongoggle's amber eyes flashed with fire and then softened. His daughters. They were his weakness, the soft marrow within his bones. He turned on his side, the bed creaking beneath his girth, and faced his wife.

"Friends?" he asked.

"A girl from down below. She's coming up tomorrow with her sisters to play." Irene held his face gently in her strong hands. "You will see, my love. At long last they will be human, too. Well"—she smiled—"human enough."

Long after his wife snored softly in her sleep, curled as

a kitten beside him, Dongoggle lay awake in bed and wondered how it had come to this. A too-soft mattress and smothering pillows? He rolled out of the bed and strolled to the window, his toenails clicking pleasantly along the stone floor. He threw open the window and leaned out as far as his bulk would allow. Nostrils flaring, he caught the unmistakable scent of every human body in the building. They were an assortment of sweet and pungent, rank and perfumed, but all alive with blood and flesh and bone. He leaned out farther, and beyond the fringes of the town that had encroached year after year upon his ancestral lands, Dongoggle found the musty odor of once-gnawed bones hidden beneath the pines. He inhaled deeply, drawing the scent of home into his mouth and under his tongue.

Then he turned away from the window in disgust. That was over. They had finished that life. He had made a promise, and Dongoggle in all his hundreds of years had never turned his back on such a vow. Give me children, giant children, he had commanded his human wife, and I will grant you whatever you wish. And she did, though the last child nearly cost her life. In gratitude, he had given Irene a precious sip from the magical Waters of Life, restoring her health, and she had arisen from her birthing bed a stronger woman. And so she had cared for their children, washed them, fed them, butchered with her broad hands whatever meat he lay before her without question, though she would eat none at all. But she fed her daughters stories of the world, too; of pretty things, of dresses and sweets, of streets with sleek horses and beetle-black carriages. She told them they were princesses, hidden away until they could be discovered by princes and showered with gold, with love. And they ate it all, eyes glistening with anticipation. Dongoggle shook his head. He should have known. When she came to him with her wish, it was not her voice that did the asking.

"Take us to the city, Papa," his daughters chorused. "We want to see it. We want a carriage ride, a dress with lace, candies. Take us to a house with servants and maids, with beds and sheets. We are human, too."

Dongoggle howled and stamped his feet. His daughters threw themselves on the ground and kicked their feet until it broke his heart to hear them. Then, without Irene ever having said a word, he agreed to take them to the city, to the human world where they would live, somehow.

"But you must not tell anyone where we are from," he warned them. "We do not have papers," he said, "and they would try and hurt us if such a thing were known." The girls did not understand why papers should matter so, for they had many fine papers, even books. But they consented, for it was enough that their wish, their mother's wish, had been answered.

"I do not like that girl Molly," Dongoggle said the next night as he heaved his bulk into bed. "She is crafty and up to no good."

"Oh nonsense," said Irene, playfully tapping his shoulder. "She's just a little girl. And isn't it wonderful to see our daughters playing with Molly and her two sisters? Three for three. I see them smile, their eyes twinkle."

"Twinkle with something dangerous," muttered Dongoggle. "Molly's eye is hungry."

"Oh, worry not, my love. They are just little girls," Irene said, and snuggled close beside him and promptly went to sleep.

But Dongoggle did not fall asleep. How had it happened that Molly and her sisters had come to spend the night, cozy in his daughters' bed? The girls had pleaded, Irene had consented, and all before he had returned home from wandering in the town, which was where he went each and every day. He did this to protect them, to create the illusion for their neighbors that he worked as human men did. But it was a burden that over the years had all but crushed his spirit. The city was no place for him, and his daily wanderings through factory smoke and city squalor, through the weed-covered parks and straggling trees, made him yearn for the biting cold of winter morning in his true home.

He twitched his ear to listen to the sound of his daughters' breathing. He heard the soft pants of Molly and her sisters, the creak of the slats as they turned in the unfamiliar comfort of the huge bed. Dongoggle closed his eyes and willed himself to sleep.

Sometime before the breaking of dawn he was sure he heard a sound; a scratching like a mouse rummaging through the covers. He growled a soft warning in the back of his throat, waited to hear more, but then fell back to sleep.

"Oh, it is gone! Gone!" cried Irene the next night at dinner. Standing on a chair, she combed the back reaches of a high shelf. "The golden bowl is missing. I used it but yesterday to give the girls a special treat of lady fingers and Turkish delights. But where did I put it?"

Dongoggle's daughters began to cry. "No more sweeties. We want our sweeties!"

Molly, Dongoggle thought as he went to calm his frantic wife. It was a trifle, a wedding gift of sorts. A golden dish that magically produced the sweetest confections the world had to offer. Irene had a tooth for these things, though Dongoggle himself cared little for such fare. Whenever they returned home to the forest he would find her another, he promised. But from the fountain of her tears, he realized she meant to stay, even if it meant the loss of her precious gift.

Dongoggle was quiet that night in bed. He recalled the mousy sounds the night before, and he did not tell Irene that he had seen Molly on the landing, leaning against her door, when he'd arrived home today. She had sneered at him, a smear of jam across her face and chocolate frosting on her chin. He smelled the butter, cream, and sugar oozing from her skin. Rich food for a poor child, he had thought. Irene would reject such an idea, claim he was being cruel to the little girl because she was human. But lying in the dark, he knew Molly had stolen the dish, though he could not imagine how she had managed the climb to the top shelf. She was a spider, he thought, creeping along the walls.

The next morning they woke to deep rolls of thunder. Rain pelted the windows as if trying to break the glass. Irene lit tapers, but even the little flames failed to push back the gloom. Dongoggle dressed in tweeds, a fur-lined greatcoat, and a stiff top hat. He carried a silver-handled umbrella and shouldered his way into the violent weather.

He walked slowly through the city, for once enjoying himself. The rain never bothered him, and he liked to see

the humans scurrying like rabbits into their warrens. Water sluiced through the city streets, carrying away the litter of these untidy animals. The dense aroma of stone, earth, and decaying wood filled his nostrils. He lingered in the park, letting the cold rain bathe his upturned face when no one was around. The storm crackled with lightning, growled with thunder, and shook the trees. He smiled for the first time in weeks.

It was late in the evening when he arrived home, slowly ascending the stairs, water dripping from his coat and hat, leaving rivulets in his wake. He tensed at the landing, expecting for a moment to see the smug face of Molly Whuppie, and then was relieved to see no one there waiting for him. He turned the key in his front door and scowled, hearing an unfamiliar giggle in the foyer. Stepping across the threshold, he saw Molly hiding behind the umbrella stand in his hallway. She put her finger to her lips, motioning him to be silent.

"What are you doing here?" he asked gruffly.

"There you are," squealed his eldest daughter, and pounced on Molly. "We're playing a game, Papa. Of hide-and-seek. And I won!"

"Your papa cheated," Molly retorted. "Not nice to cheat. Spoils the fun for others, it does. You must let me hide again."

His daughter pouted, began to cry, and Molly, fists curled, relented. But as she headed down the hall to the girls' bedroom, she cast a glance full of malice over her shoulder at Dongoggle. "Cheaters get punished," she muttered.

Dongoggle strode angrily into the kitchen to find Irene. She was sitting at the table, her chin resting in her upturned palm and staring glumly into her teacup. She didn't look up when he entered, even though he snarled and smacked the wet top hat on the table.

"Why is that girl here?" he demanded.

"Oh, let them play. They're just little girls," Irene said peevishly. "I couldn't find the heart to amuse the girls myself today. I miss my little dish, my gift from you," she said, and looked up at him with melancholy eyes. "I can't imagine where it went."

"I will get you another," he said, and she brightened, "when we return to the forest," and he watched her face crumple again.

"I don't want to go there. I like it here," she said.

Dongoggle harrumphed. A vow was a vow, and he could not break it. But he longed to crack the bones of Molly Whuppie and suck out the bitter marrow. He promised himself that he would be vigilant that night. That nothing would happen.

But Dongoggle was tired. He had walked a great distance in the bracing air of the storm and was weary in his bones. Sniffing back tears, Irene fed him his dinner, golden plates filled with steaming victuals. He ate his fill, hoping it would help rouse him, but once sated, his eyes grew heavy, the lids closing. He struggled weakly against his fatigue, but offered little resistance when Irene helped him to his bed at last. She unbuttoned his tweed coat, pulling from his pockets his possessions: a gold watch and fob, a small leather pouch, and a knife neatly folded in a case. She pulled off his trousers, heavy with rain, and rolled him tenderly into the bed. Dongoggle fell immediately into a deep and dreamless sleep.

Yet he awoke at dawn, a light clinking sound twisting his ear. He sat up in bed as something small scurried from the room and down the hall. The key turned in the lock and the front door opened. He bolted from the bed, his nightshirt swaddled around his trunk legs and slowing him down. By the time he had reached the top landing and peered down, he saw the back of Molly Whuppie, rushing her sisters down the stairs to their apartment below. She heard him on the landing and looked up with an evil smile in the half light.

"I'll get you, Molly Whuppie," he whispered hoarsely.

She laughed and shouted back. "Nyah, nyah. You've nothing on me, but I've the goods on you. It's back to

Spain where you came from, old sod . . . and your girls to the gutter, for all I care."

"Who's that up there making a racket?" hollered an angry voice from the floor below. At once a baby started squalling, a dog barked, and more protesting voices joined the chorus. Dongoggle withdrew into the apartment, not wanting to draw any further attention to himself. As he shut the door, he decided that he could no longer ignore the threat to his family and himself. Molly Whuppie would destroy them if she could. It didn't matter that they had done nothing to her. Or that for almost a century they had kept quietly to themselves, and he had not taken a single life in all that time but had endured the secondhand death of slaughtered livestock, bland and tasteless to his palate. A vow was a vow, and he could not change that. But he could conceive of a way in which to rid himself of Molly Whuppie without breaking his vow.

He dressed quickly that morning, saying nothing to his wife nor his sleeping daughters. As he scooped the knife and gold watch and fob off the night table and into his pocket, he realized what Molly Whuppie had stolen from him: his pouch of never-ending coins. It had been a gift from his father, passed down from father to son since the world was new and their kind ruled. The leather was from the hide of a manticore, and the coins were exhaled from the metallic dust of the universe. Each time the pouch was opened, it was filled with coins anew. Dongoggle snarled. The pouch was also the source of their wealth. It paid for everything. Without it, there was no other way to survive, for Dongoggle's pride was such that he would not labor as a son of Adam. His kind was older than that and would not suffer such indignity. There were still treasures left that could be sold, but piece by piece they would lose their heritage, their history, along with their wealth.

Dongoggle drew on his coat and strode briskly down the stairs and out into the fog-covered morning. The dampness touched his cheek and he knew, ere he returned home that night, he would have a plan to rid them of Molly Whuppie forever.

It was late in the evening, the streets abandoned except for stray cats, when Dongoggle returned home. And yet, as he entered his home he heard again the gay laughter of his daughters and of Molly Whuppie and her sisters. He smiled in spite of his silent rage. Irene met him in the hallway to take his coat and hat. She looked apologetic.

"I could not say no to our daughters. They begged so prettily that Molly and her sisters might come and play. And how they talk and tell stories! I have tried to quiet them, but they are too excited to sleep."

"It doesn't matter tonight, Irene," he said gruffly. "Let them play this last time together."

Dongoggle retrieved from his pocket strands of rye grass twisted and braided into three necklaces. He pushed open the door to his daughters' bedroom and forced a smile at the sight of the six girls sitting in a circle on the bed. They were leaning close, clutching each other in mock fright as Molly Whuppie regaled them with a terror tale. "And then the giant grabbed the little girl by the neck—" She scowled as soon as she saw him.

Dongoggle composed himself and approached the girls. "Here," he said, handing Molly and her sisters the braided rye-grass necklaces. "I've brought these for you. I thought you might like them. Put them on and let's see how they look."

"Oh Papa, how pretty," said his youngest daughter. "They look like our necklaces."

"Yours are gold," sniffed Molly. "I too will have gold necklaces. One day soon."

"But they are still pretty! Put them on! Put them on!" his daughters cried.

Molly and her sisters put on the necklaces.

"Now you look like us!" said his middle daughter.

Dongoggle saw the sly gleam in Molly's eyes as the girl twisted her fingers through the hem of her threadbare nightdress.

That night, Dongoggle waited until the house was quiet, settled in deep sleep. He listened for the sounds of his daughters breathing, the little panted breaths of Molly and her sisters, and the soft snores of his wife. When he was certain that he was the only one awake, he left his bed and padded quietly down the halls. Over his shoulder he carried a sack and a rope.

Dongoggle slipped quietly into his daughters' room and went to stand at the head of the bed. In the darkness he reached over the bedstead and felt for the grass necklace of the first girl. As soon as his fingers touched it, he closed one hand around her neck and the other firmly over her mouth, then lifted the struggling girl and dumped her into the sack. He knocked her out with a thump of his fist to her temple, and went for the second girl. It had happened so quickly, so quietly, that the other sleepers on the bed scarcely moved a muscle in their sleep. Swiftly, he gathered up the other two girls with necklaces of straw and placed them in the sack and tied the rope around the top.

He crept out of his daughters' room again, pleased with himself that he had accomplished his task without so much as a sound or a turning of the sleepers still in the bed. With the sack on his shoulder, he walked over to the parlor windows and opened wide the casements. Dongoggle whispered an old spell into the night as the wind rose and billowed the curtains. Hoisting the sack over the window ledge, he tossed it into the mouth of the wind where it disappeared with its sleeping cargo. Satisfied, Dongoggle shut the casement and returned to his bed.

Dongoggle woke when the first red rays of sunrise pierced the lingering morning fog. He dressed quickly, eager for once to be on his way. He glanced at his wife, still sleeping, curled in the coverlet. He placed a bowler on his head, slipped out of the front door, and headed down the stairs.

On the landing below he stopped, and the raw metallic taste of blood filled his mouth. Molly Whuppie waited for him, leaning on the railing, her fingers twirling a gold chain. With a throttled cry, Dongoggle lunged at her, grabbing her around the neck in his huge hands. He lifted her high in the air and opened wide his maw. The thick red tongue rolled out between his fangs. He would crush her, a single bite, and her face, that smug sneering smile, would be gone. What did it matter anymore?

She screamed, her hands vainly plucking at his thick fingers on her neck. She kicked out hard, but her legs could find no purchase. He brought her face close to his so that he could see the terror in her rolling eyes. But though she screamed, he saw not terror but envy, greed, and worst of all, a triumphant rage.

In that instant he heard Irene's wailing from the apartment above. And from the street below, the shrill sounds of a police whistle. Molly's screams turned to choked laughter. Dongoggle dropped her, understanding at last what she had done. Not only had she switched the necklaces in the night, tricking him into harming his own daughters, but she had then called the police to come and take him away. No time to waste. He bolted up the stairs to Irene.

"Go away then with you. Go back to Spain, where'er it is you come from. You'll not get the better of me!" Molly crowed after him. "You've no rights to be here." She followed him up the stairs. "No papers, no papers . . . You're dirty, thieving, and you'll go to prison now. You're trapped, old sod."

Dongoggle had stopped listening to Molly's threats. His ears twitched to the sounds of dogs baying, the shrill whistles, and his wife's wailing shattering the morning. He ran into their apartment throwing off the bowler hat, the confining tweed coat, and the stiff, collared shirt. He found Irene in his daughters' bedroom tearing at the sheets as though she expected to discover them still hiding amidst the covers.

"My daughters are gone. They're gone," she sobbed.

"I will take you to them," he growled. "Come, Irene, we must go." He held out his hand to her, palm up, the long ivory claws stained with the bloody sunrise.

She hesitated, tensed like a deer too terrified to move.

"Come," he said more gently so as not frighten her. "Our daughters are waiting."

She reached for him then. He took her hand and swung her effortlessly across his back. She clasped her legs around his waist, her arms clinging to his broad neck. The police clamored up the stairs, the dogs howling to be let go. With Irene on his back, Dongoggle crashed through the window of the top floor and fell down and down and down to the street below.

He landed in a crouch and felt the sidewalk give way as cracks exploded around his feet. Startled onlookers drew back, shouting or screaming. Men attacked him with cobblestones. On his back Irene sobbed and clutched him tighter. Dongoggle met their attacks, batting them away with a swing of his powerful arm. He sent them crashing into walls, or tossed them over the pointed spires of the wrought-iron fences. Freed of them, Dongoggle ducked his head and ran down the narrow city streets, away from the screams and shouts, away from the police whistle and baying dogs, and most of all, away from Molly Whuppie's mocking laughter.

From city to the low-lying farms he ran, spurred by the knowledge of what had happened to his daughters. He would not rest until he had arrived home again, deep in the forest, and found the ruined stones of his castle. His daughters were there, no doubt having awoken from their slumber to discover themselves imprisoned in a sack. And even if they succeeded in freeing themselves, they would be alone in the darkness of an underground crypt, the only structure still intact below the castle ruins. It was to have been Molly's fate, for his vow forbade him from killing her or any human while they lived in the city—but nothing was promised about leaving them where they might be eaten by other creatures or starve. But now, Dongoggle could not bear the thought of his daughters waking to that solitary horror, surrounded by the monstrous skeletons of their unknown ancestors.

Soon, he thought, hoisting the sleeping Irene higher on his back. *Soon*, he whispered, reaching his body through the wall of mist circling the trees at the edge of the forest. *Soon*, the feathery branches brushed against his cheek in a welcome home. *Soon*, he would find his daughters, and never more would they leave the forest.

Midori Snyder is the author of the young adult novel *Hannah's Garden* and the fantasy trilogy which includes *New Moon, Sadar's Keep,* and *Beldan's Fire.* She lives in Wisconsin and likes to write in libraries.

Midori says: "When I was young, Molly seemed so heroic against the giant. I admired her bravery as she outwitted him, not once but three times. But as I grew older, I wondered about the fairness of it all. Yes, giants can be flesh-chomping creatures. But this giant was minding his own business when Molly arrived at his home. Before she is done with him, Molly steals from him, tricks him into beating his wife and strangling his daughters, and then mocks him when he chases after her.

So who is *really* the monster? Was Molly jealous of the giant's daughters because their parents loved them? Was she greedy because she thought he was only a monster and didn't deserve his wealth? Did she hate the giant and his human wife because they were different from the people she knew? I thought about those questions and wondered how it would it be if the giant had a chance to tell *his* side of their encounter."

Observing the Formalities

Neil Gaiman

As you know, I wasn't invited to the Christening. Get
over it, you repeat.
But it's the little formalities that keep the world
turning.
My twelve sisters each had an invitation, engraved,
and delivered
By a footman. I thought perhaps my footman had got
lost.

Few invitations reach me here. People no longer leave
visiting cards.
And even when they did, I would tell them I was not
at home,
Deploring the unmannerliness of these more recent
generations.
They eat with their mouths open. They interrupt.

Manners are all, and the formalities. When we lose those
We have lost everything. Without them, we might as well be dead.
Dull, useless things. The young should be taught a trade, should hew or spin,
Should know their place and stick to it. Be seen, not heard. Be hushed.

My youngest sister invariably is late, and interrupts. I am myself a stickler for punctuality.
I told her, no good will come of being late. I told her,
Back when we were still speaking, when she was still listening. She laughed.
It could be argued that I should not have turned up uninvited.

But people must be taught lessons. Without them, none of them will ever learn.
People are dreams and awkwardness and gawk. They prick their fingers
Bleed and snore and drool. Politeness is as quiet as a grave,

Unmoving, roses without thorns. Or white lilies.
    People have to learn.

Inevitably my sister turned up late. Punctuality is the
    politeness of princes,
That, and inviting all potential godmothers to a
    Christening.
They said they thought I was dead. Perhaps I am. I
    can no longer recall.
Still and all, it was necessary to observe the
    formalities.

I would have made her future so tidy and polite.
    Eighteen is old enough. More than enough.
After that, life gets so messy. Loves and hearts are
    such untidy things.
Christenings are raucous times and loud, and
    rancorous,
As bad as weddings. Invitations go astray. We'd argue
    about precedence and gifts.

They would have invited me to the funeral.

Neil Gaiman has written books and comics and films and songs. He lives in a big old house on one side of the Atlantic or the other. He has lots of awards, several cats, and a large white dog.

Neil says: "I always wondered about the fairies in 'Sleeping Beauty,' and that final, late fairy, changing death into sleep. It's all about gifts, after all, and etiquette. I'm not quite sure why that transmuted into a poem. . . ."

The Cinderella Game
Kelly Link

One day Peter would have his own secret hideaway just like this one, his stepfather's forbidden room, up in the finished attic: leather couches, stereo system with speakers the size of school lockers, flat-screen television, and so many horror movies you'd be able to watch a different one every night of the year. The movie Peter picked turned out to be in a foreign language, but it was still pretty scary, and there were werewolves in it.

"What are you doing?" someone said. Peter spilled popcorn all over the couch.

His new stepsister, Darcy, stood in the door that went down to the second floor. Her hair was black and knotted and stringy, and, no surprise, she was wearing one of her dozens of princess dresses. This one had been pink and spangled at one point. Now it looked like something a zombie would wear to a fancy dress party.

"What are you doing up here?" Peter saw, with fascinated horror, the greasy smears left behind on the leather as he chased popcorn back into the bowl. "Go away. Why aren't you asleep?"

His stepsister said, "Dad says I'm not allowed to watch scary movies." She'd holstered a fairy wand in the pocket of her princess gown. The battered tiara on her head was missing most of its rhinestones.

You are *a scary movie*, Peter thought. "How long have you been standing here?"

"Not long. Since the werewolf bit the other lady. You were picking your nose."

It got better and better. "If you're not allowed to watch scary movies, then what are you doing up here?"

"What are you doing up here?" Darcy said. "We're not supposed to watch television up here without an adult. Why aren't you in bed? Where's Mrs. Daly?"

"She had to go home. Somebody called and said her husband was in the hospital. Mom hasn't come back yet," Peter said. "So I'm in charge until they get home. She and your dad are still out on their we-won't-go-on-a-honeymoon-we'll-just-have-a-mini-honeymoon-every-Monday-night-for-the-rest-of-our-lives special date. Apparently there was a wait at the restaurant, blah blah blah, and so they're going to a later movie. They called and I said that Mrs. Daly was in the bathroom. So just go back to bed, okay?"

"You're not my babysitter," his stepsister said. "You're only three years older than me."

"Four and a half years older," he said. "So you have to do what I say. If I told you to go jump in a fire then you'd have to jump. Got it?"

"I'm not a baby," Darcy said. But she was. She was only eight.

One of the movie werewolves was roaming through a house, playing hide-and-seek. There were puddles of blood everywhere. It came into a room where there was a parrot, reached up with a humanlike paw, and opened the door of the cage. Peter and Darcy both watched for a minute, and then Peter said, "You *are* a baby. You have over a hundred stuffed animals. You know all the words to all the songs from *The Little Mermaid*. My mom told me you still wet the bed."

"Why are you so mean?" She said it like she was actually curious.

Peter addressed the werewolves. "How can I explain this so that someone your age will understand? I'm not mean. I'm just honest. It's not like I'm your real brother. We just happen to live in the same house, because your father needed someone to do his taxes, and my mother is a certified accountant. The rest of it I don't even pretend to understand." Although he did. Her father was rich. His mother wasn't. "Okay? Now go to bed."

"No." Darcy did a little dance, as if to demonstrate that she could do whatever she wanted.

"Fine," he said. "Stay here and watch the werewolf movie then."

"I don't want to."

"Then go play princess or whatever it is you're always doing." Darcy had a closet with just princess dresses in it. And tiaras. And fairy wands. And fairy wings.

"You play with me," she said. "Or I'll tell everyone you pick your nose."

"Who cares," Peter said. "Go away."

"I'll pay you."

"How much?" he said, just out of curiosity.

"Ten dollars."

He thought for a minute. Her grandparents had given her a check for her birthday. Little kids never knew what to do with money, and as far as he could tell, her father bought her everything she wanted anyway. And she got an allowance. Peter got one now too, of course, but he'd knocked a glass of orange juice over on his laptop, and his mom said she was only going to pay for half of what a new one would cost. "Make it fifty."

"Twenty," Darcy said. She came over and sat on the couch beside him. She smelled awful. A rank, feral smell, like something that lived in a cave. He'd heard his stepfather tell his mother that half the time Darcy only ran the water and then splashed it around with her hands behind a locked door. Make-believe baths, which was funny when you thought about how much she worshipped Ariel from *The Little Mermaid*. When Darcy really took a bath she left a ring of grime around the tub. He'd seen it with his own eyes.

Peter said, "What does this involve, exactly?"

"We could play Three Little Pigs. Or Cinderella. You be the evil stepsister."

Like everything was already decided. Just to annoy her, Peter said, "For a lousy twenty bucks I get to be whoever I want. I'm Cinderella. You can be the evil stepsister."

"You can't be Cinderella!"

"Why not?"

"Because you're a boy."

"So what?"

Darcy seemed to have no answer to this. She examined the hem of her princess dress. Pulled a few remaining sequins off, as if they were scabs. Finally she said, "My dad says I have to be nice to you. Because this is really my house, and you're a guest, even though I didn't invite you to come live here, and now you're going to live here all the time and never go away unless you die or get sent away to military school or something."

"Don't count on it," Peter said, feeling really annoyed now. So that was his stepfather's plan. Or maybe it was his mother, still working out the details of her new, perfect life, worrying that Peter was going to mess things up now that she'd gotten it. He'd gone in and out of three schools in the last two years. It was easy enough to get thrown out of school if you wanted to be. If they sent him away, he'd come right back. "Maybe I like it here."

Darcy looked at him suspiciously. It wasn't like she was problem free, either. She went to see a therapist every Tuesday to deal with some "abandonment issues," which were apparently due to the fact that her real mother now lived in Hawaii.

Peter said, "I'm Cinderella. Deal with it."

His stepsister shrugged. She said, "If I'm the evil stepsister then I get to tell you what to do. First you have to go put the toilet seat down in the bathroom. And I get to hold the remote and you have to go to bed first. And you have to cry a lot. And sing. And make me a peanut butter sandwich with no crusts. And a bowl of chocolate ice cream. And I get your PlayStation, because Cinderella doesn't get to have any toys."

"I've changed my mind," Peter said, when she seemed to have finished. He grinned at her. *My what big teeth I have.* "I'm going to be the *evil* Cinderella."

She bared her teeth right back at him. "Wrong. Cinderella isn't evil. She gets to go to the ball and wear a princess dress. And mice like her."

"Cinderella might be evil," Peter said, thinking it through, remembering how it went in the Disney movie. Everybody treated Cinderella like she was a pushover. Didn't she sleep in a fireplace? "If her evil stepsister keeps making fun of her and taking away her PlayStation, she might burn down the house with everyone in it."

"That isn't how the story goes. This is stupid," Darcy said. She was beginning to sound less sure of herself, however.

"This is the new, improved version. No fairy godmother. No prince. No glass slipper. No happy ending. Better run away, Darcy. Because evil Cinderella is coming to get you." Peter stood up. Loomed over Darcy in what he hoped was a menacing way. The werewolves were howling on the TV.

Darcy shrank back into the couch. Held up her fairy wand as if it would keep her safe. "No, wait! You have to count to one hundred first. And I'll go hide."

Peter grabbed the stupid, cheap wand. Pointed it at Darcy's throat. Tapped it on her chest and when she looked down, bounced it off her nose. "I'll count to ten. Unless you want to pay me another ten bucks. Then I'll count higher."

"I only have five more dollars!" Darcy protested.

"You got fifty bucks from your grandparents last weekend."

"Your mom made me put half of it into a savings account."

"Okay. I'll count to twenty-three." He put the werewolf movie on pause. "One."

He went into all the bedrooms on the second floor, flicking the light switches on and off. She wasn't under any of the beds. Or in the closets. Or behind the shower curtain in the show-off master bathroom. Or in either of the other two bathrooms on the second floor. He couldn't believe how many bathrooms there were in this house. Back in the dark hallway again he saw something and paused. It was a mirror, and he was in it. He paused to look at himself. No Cinderella here. Something dangerous. Something out of place. He felt a low, wild, wolfish delight rise up in him. His mother looked at him sometimes as if she wasn't sure who he was. He wasn't sure, either. He had to look away from what he saw in the face in the mirror.

Wasn't there some other fairy tale? *I'll huff and I'll puff and I'll blow your house down.* He'd like to blow this house down. The first time his mother had brought him over for dinner, she'd said, "Well, what do you think?" in the car, as they came up the driveway. What he'd thought was that it was like television. He'd never seen a house like it except on TV. There had been two forks at dinner and a white cloth napkin he was afraid to use in case he got it dirty. Some kind of vegetable that he didn't even recognize, and macaroni and cheese that didn't taste right. He'd chewed with his mouth open on purpose, and the little girl across the table watched him the whole time.

Everyone was always watching him. Waiting for him to mess up. Even his friends at his last school had acted sometimes like they thought was crazy. Egged him on and then went silent when he didn't punk out. No friends yet at this new school. No bad influences, his mother said. A new start. But she was the one who had changed. Said things like, "I always wanted a little girl and now I've got one!" And, "It will be good for you, having a little sister. You're a role model now, Peter, believe it or not, so try to act like one."

Peter's mother let Darcy climb into bed with her and her new husband. Lay on the floor of the living room with her head in her new husband's lap. Darcy curled up beside them. Pretending to be a family, but he knew better. He could see the way Darcy wrinkled her nose when his mother hugged her. As if she smelled something bad, which was ironic, considering.

Peter went down the stairs two at a time. That black tide of miserable joy rose higher still, the way it always did when he knew he was doing exactly the wrong thing. As if he were going to die of it, whatever it was that he was becoming.

Darcy wasn't in the laundry room. Or the dining room. Peter went into the kitchen next, and knew immediately that she was here. Could feel her here, somewhere, holding her breath, squeezing her eyes shut, picking at her sequins. He thought of the babysitter, Mrs. Daly, and how afraid she'd looked when she left. Almost wished that she hadn't left, or that his mother and stepfather had skipped the movie, come home when they were supposed to. Wished that he'd told them about Mrs. Daly, except that his mother had sounded as if she were having a good time. As if she were happy.

He kicked a chair at the kitchen table and almost jumped out of his skin to hear it crash on the floor. Stomped around, throwing open the cabinet doors. Howling tunelessly, just for effect, except that it wasn't just for effect. He was enjoying himself. For a moment he didn't really even want to find his stepsister. Maybe no one would ever see her again.

She was folded up under the kitchen sink. Scrambled out when the door was flung open, and slapped his leg when he tried to grab her. Then scooted away on her hands and knees across the floor. There was a sort of sting in his calf now and he looked down and saw a fork was sticking out of him. It looked funny there. The tines hadn't gone far in, but still there were four little holes in the fabric of his jeans. Around the four little holes the black jeans turned blacker. Now it hurt.

"You stabbed me!" Peter said. He almost laughed. "With a fork!"

"I'm the evil stepsister," his stepsister said, glaring at him. "Of course I stabbed you. I'll stab you again if you don't do what I say."

"With what, a spoon?" he said. "You are going to be in so much trouble."

"I don't care," Darcy said. "Evil stepsisters don't care about getting in trouble." She stood up and straightened her princess dress. Then she walked over and gave him a little furious shove. Not such a little shove. He staggered back and then lurched forward again. Swung out for balance, and hit her across her middle with the back of one hand. Maybe he did it on purpose, but he didn't *think* he'd meant to do it. Either way the result was terrible. Blow your house down. Darcy was flung back across the room like she was just a piece of paper.

Now I've done it, he thought. Now they really will

send me away. Felt a howling rage so enormous and hurtful that he gasped out loud. He darted after her, bent over her, and grabbed a shoulder. Shook it hard. Darcy's head flopped back and hit the refrigerator door, and she made a little noise. "You made me," he said. "Not my fault. If you tell them—"

And stopped. "My mother is going to—" he said, and then had to stop again. He let go of Darcy. He couldn't imagine what his mother would do.

He knelt down. Saw his own blood smeared on the tiles. Not much. His leg felt warm. Darcy looked up at him, her ratty hair all in her face. She had her pajama bottoms on under that stupid dress. She was holding one arm with the other, like maybe he'd broken it. She didn't cry or yell at him and her eyes were enormous and black. Probably she had a concussion. Maybe they'd run into Mrs. Daly and her husband when they went to the hospital. He felt like throwing up.

"I don't know what I'm supposed to do!" he said. It came out in a roar. He didn't even know what he meant. "I don't know what I'm doing here! Tell me what I'm doing here."

Darcy stared at him. She seemed astonished. "You're Peter," she said. "You're being my stepbrother."

"Your evil stepbrother," he said, and forced out a laugh,

trying to make it a joke. But it was a wild, evil laugh.

Darcy got up, rubbing her head. She swung her other arm in a way that suggested it wasn't broken after all. He tried to feel relieved about this, but instead he just felt guiltier. He could think of no way to make things better, and so he did nothing. He watched while Darcy went over and picked up the fork where he'd dropped it, carried it over to the sink, and then stood on the footstool to rinse it off. She looked over at him. Said with a shrug, "They're home."

Car lights bounced against the windows.

His stepsister got down off the stool. She had a wet sponge in her hand. Calmly she crouched down and scrubbed at the bloody tiles. Swiped once at the blood on his jeans, and then gave up. Went back to the sink, stopping to pick up and straighten the chair he'd knocked over, and ran the water again to get the blood out of the sponge while he just sat and watched.

His mother came in first. She was laughing, probably at something his stepfather had said. His stepfather was always making jokes. It was one of the things Peter hated most about his stepfather, how he could make his mother laugh so easily. And how quickly her face would change from laughter, when she talked to Peter, or like now, when she looked over and saw Darcy at the sink, Peter on the floor. His stepfather came in right behind her, still saying something funny, his mouth invisible behind that bearish, bluish-blackish beard. He was holding a doggy bag.

"Peter," his mother said, knowing right away, the way she always did. "What's going on?"

He opened up his mouth to explain everything, but Darcy got there first. She ran over and hugged his mother around the legs. Lucky for his mother she wasn't holding a fork. And now here it came, the end of everything.

"Mommy," Darcy said, and Peter could see the magical effect this one word had, even on accountants. How his mother grew rigid with surprise, then lovingly pliant, as if Darcy had injected her with some kind of muscle relaxant.

Darcy turned her head, still holding his mother in that monstrously loving hold, and gave Peter a look he didn't understand until she began to speak in a rush. "Mommy, it was Cinderella because I couldn't sleep and Mrs. Daly had to go home and I woke up and we were waiting for you to come home and I got scared. Don't be angry. Peter and I were just playing a game. I was the evil stepsister." Again she looked at Peter.

"And I was Cinderella," Peter said. The leg of his pants was stiff with blood, but he could come up with an explanation tomorrow if only Darcy continued to keep his mother distracted. He had to get upstairs before anyone else. Get changed into his pajamas. Put things away in the forbidden room, where the werewolves waited patiently in the dark for their story to begin again. To begin the game again. No one could see what was in Darcy's face right now but him. He wished she would look away. He saw that she still had a smear of his blood on her hand, from the sponge, and she glanced down and saw it, too. Slowly, still looking at Peter, she wiped her hand against the princess dress until there was nothing left to see.

Kelly Link is the author of three collections: *Magic for Beginners, Stranger Things Happen,* and *Pretty Monsters.* Her short stories have appeared in *A Wolf at the Door and Other Retold Fairy Tales; Noisy Outlaws, Unfriendly Blobs, and Some Other Things; Firebirds Rising; The Starry Rift; The Coyote Road: Trickster Tales;* and *The Restless Dead.* When she gets stuck, she goes to Holly Black for story advice. She and her husband, Gavin J. Grant, live in Northampton, Massachusetts, which is only a short drive away from the Eric Carle Museum.

Kelly says: "As I began to write this story, I quickly realized that everyone in it could be a villain. It just depends on which fairy tale you think you're reading. My favorite fairy-tale villains are the wolf from 'Little Red Riding Hood' and the servant girl who switches places with the princess in 'The Goose Girl.' I also love 'Mr. Fox' and the advice that his bride-to-be sees carved above the door to his house: BE BOLD, BE BOLD. She goes inside, of course, and then she sees more advice: BE BOLD, BE BOLD, BUT NOT TOO BOLD. But she goes through that door, too. The next piece of advice is BE BOLD, BE BOLD, BUT NOT TOO BOLD, LEST THAT YOUR HEART'S BLOOD RUN COLD. I bet you can imagine what she does anyway."

Further Reading

Some Good Fairy-Tale Collections

Strange Things Sometimes Still Happen, edited by Angela
Carter
The Classic Fairy Tales, edited by Maria Tatar
Favorite Folktales from Around the World, edited by Jane
Yolen
Spells of Enchantment, edited by Jack Zipes

Some Good Fairy-Tale Novels for Middle-Grade and
Young-Adult Readers

The Phoenix Dance by Dia Calhoun
The Mirror's Tale (and other novels) by P. W. Catanese
Roses by Barbara Cohen
Wolf by Gillian Cross
The Glass Slipper by Eleanor Farjeon
The Seventh Swan by Nicholas Stuart Gray
The Goose Girl by Shannon Hale
Mira, Mirror by Mette Ivie Harrison
Waking by Alyxandra Harvey-Fitzhenry

The Snow Queen by Eileen Kernaghan

Goose Chase by Patrice Kindl

Thumbelina by Andrea Koenig

Ella Enchanted (and other novels) by Gail Carson Levine

Mirror, Mirror by Gregory Maguire

Birdwing by Rafe Martin

Malkin by Sophie Masson

Spindle's End (and other novels) by Robin McKinley

Zel (and other novels) by Donna Jo Napoli

East by Edith Pattou

I Was a Rat! by Philip Pullman

Kindergarten by Peter Rushford

Straw into Gold by Gary D. Schmidt

Bella at Midnight by Diane Stanley

Swan's Wing by Ursula Synge

Briar Rose by Jane Yolen

Fairy Tales Online

The Sur la Lune Fairy Tale Pages,
edited by Heidi Anne Heiner:
www.surlalunefairytales.com

Ellen Datlow fondly remembers her mother reading Oscar Wilde's tragic fairy tales to her under a tree one summer in the Bronx, where she lived until she was eight years old. She continued to devour fairy tales on her own as a young adult and adult and became an editor of science fiction, fantasy, and horror. She was fiction editor of OMNI Magazine and of SCI FICTION, part of the Web site for the SCI FI Channel.

Ellen has edited and coedited many anthologies, including the Snow White, Blood Red adult fairy-tale series; the series of young adult anthologies including *The Green Man, The Faery Reel,* and *The Coyote Road*; *Salon Fantastique* (all with Terri Windling); and the annual *The Year's Best Fantasy and Horror* (through number sixteen). She has won eight World Fantasy Awards, two Bram Stoker Awards, four *Locus* Awards, three Hugo Awards, and the International Horror Guild Award for her editing, and was named recipient of the 2007 Karl Edward Wagner Award, given at the British Fantasy Convention for "outstanding contribution to the genre."

She lives in Manhattan's Greenwich Village with two demanding but terrific cats.

Her Web site is www.datlow.com.

Terri Windling is a writer, painter, and editor who lives in Devon, England. She has loved fairy tales ever since she read *The Golden Book of Fairy Tales*, illustrated by Adrienne Ségur, when she was a child.

Her favorite tale is "Donkeyskin," where the heroine who flees her home proves to be courageous, clever, and compassionate. The villain in the story is the girl's own father. Sometimes real life is like that, too.

Terri has published over thirty anthologies, including the ones coedited with Ellen Datlow listed on the previous page. She is the author of five children's books (*A Midsummer Night's Faery Tale*, *The Winter Child*, *The Faeries of Spring Cottage*, *The Changeling*, and *The Raven Queen*) and one adult novel (*The Wood Wife*). She has won eight World Fantasy Awards, the Mythopoeic Award, and the Bram Stoker Award, and has been short-listed for the Tiptree Award. Visit her online at www.terriwindling.com.